YOUNG, GIFTED AND DEADLY

A Brough and Miller investigation

William Stafford

Book Eight from the *Brough and Miller* Series

Young, Gifted and Deadly
Published in 2016 by
Acorn Books
www.acornbooks.co.uk
an imprint of
Andrews UK Limited
www.andrewsuk.com

YOUNG, GIFTED AND DEADLY

1.

"I don't think we should be doing this after dark."

Callum Phillips hung back. The others, Logger, Dogger and Bonk, were already squeezing through the gap in the railings. Years of use had created a space, a distortion in the otherwise vertical plane. It was a bit like those pictures, Callum thought, the ones I can never see.

"I knew it was a fucking mistake, bringing him," Logger spat in the general direction of Callum's smart black shoes. "Fucking pussy."

"Don't be like that, Log," said Dogger. "Cal's all right. Besides, we need him, don't we?"

Logger scowled. There was no arguing with that. Callum Phillips might be a fucking pussy but he was also Priory High School's shit-hot computer whizz kid. He was king of the nerds. Not that his I.T. skills would be called upon that evening. But soon. They wouldn't be bringing him into their intimate circle if it wasn't absolutely necessary. There was too much at stake.

"Actually," the shit-hot whizz kid was still dithering, "I think I'll just go home. I can get a bus around the corner."

Logger sneered. Typical, said that sneer. Just what you'd expect from a kid whose parents were actually married – to each other! And who owned the house they lived in and had a car each and went on skiing holidays instead of having Christmas at home in Dedley like normal people.

Logger's was a very eloquent sneer.

"Come on, Cal," Dogger urged. It was a matter of pride to him. He had spent half a term sidling up to the nerd, telling him dirty jokes (most of which Callum didn't get – nor, to tell the truth, did

Dogger) in exchange for help with his Maths homework. Dogger had taken to sitting near Callum during Lunch and making him laugh in the school's library by holding up crude and rudimentary caricatures of the teaching staff. He had got into the habit of walking the bespectacled boffin to his bus stop.

Shit; it was like they were friends or something.

Callum shrugged. An apology. He turned his back on the fence and found himself face to fist with Bonk's right hand. Bonk didn't speak. He didn't need to.

"Er—" said Callum, looking to Dogger for assistance.

"Get through that cowin' fence now!" Logger commanded.

"It's all right, Cal," Dogger offered a weak smile. "We do this all the time."

He went through the gap and came back out again to demonstrate how easy it was.

"Now!" Logger insisted. Callum stepped lively; he didn't want a fleck of the older boy's spittle to land on his blazer. He followed Dogger through the gap. "Get a move on!" Logger snapped. "Look at him. Thinks he's going to fucking Narnia. Specky twat."

He gave the specky twat a shove in the small of his back. "What's he wearing his uniform for? Didn't you tell him to wear a hoodie, Dog?"

Callum answered for himself. "I told my mum I was meeting some school chums and she asked where, and so I said at the school. She made me put on a clean shirt."

The other boys stared at him.

"You said what?" Logger's blood was beginning to boil. "You told your mom you was coming here?"

"I'm not in the habit of lying to my parents."

"Fucking hell," said Dogger.

"You've got more than one shirt?" said Bonk.

"Where's your fucking hoodie?" Logger stabbed the specky twat's striped tie with his finger.

2

"I don't have one," said Callum. "Sorry."

This was the most incredible revelation. A fourteen-year-old boy who didn't have a hooded jacket?

"Did you lose it?" said Bonk, his square face cragged with pity.

"I told you this was a fucking mistake," said Logger. "How's he expected to be a Monk without a hoodie?"

"A what?" Callum's eyes blinked behind his prescription lenses.

"He can get one when he passes the test," hissed Dogger.

Callum brightened. "Test? Is it written?"

"Fuck me," said Logger. "Should've let him fuck off home."

The three hooded youths frogmarched Callum away from the fence and across the playing field. Callum cringed at every step, concerned about the mud caking his best school shoes but he deemed it prudent not to let his discomfort show on his face. Not that they were paying him much attention. Dogger would cast an occasional glance over his shoulder while Logger and Bonk brought up the rear. They arrived at a row of bushes that ran along another, much shorter fence, the dividing line between the school field and the municipal car park beyond.

"Here we are," Dogger announced, coming to a halt. Callum looked around. Ahead, the yellow sodium glare of the car park lighting revealed an empty lot; behind, only the security lights of the school buildings. The school overlooked the field from an embankment. It loomed dark against the evening sky – like a haunted house on a cliff, thought Callum. The boys had skirted the farthest edge of the field in order not to trigger the full blare of the lights and be frozen in brightness like cartoon characters escaping from prison.

"What now?" Callum directed the question at Dogger, the most amenable of the trio.

"We wait," said Dogger, his face alive with a delightful secret.

"We wait; you watch," said Logger, evidently in on the secret.

"Yeah," added Bonk.

"Watch what?" said Callum. Despite his misgivings, he was keen to impress the uncouth youths; Dogger was the closest thing Callum had to a friend.

"Ssh!" said Dogger, raising a finger to his lips.

"You'll see," said Logger, with undertones of menace.

"Yeah," said Bonk.

"But first, give's your phone." Logger held out his hand.

"I will do no such thing!" Callum cried. There are limits.

"Give's it! There's no selfies allowed."

"You'll get it back," Dogger encouraged. "He'll get it back, won't he, Log?"

"Yeah," said Bonk. He took a step closer to Callum, who took a step back, only to have a branch of a bush poke him in the blazer.

"All right!" He took out his smartphone and handed it to Dogger, who whistled in appreciation.

"Not bad," he said.

"You must be loaded," said Logger, as though accusing the specky twat of rancid flatulence.

"Actually, I paid for that myself," said Callum. "From my paper round."

"Christ," said Logger. "Your parents must be minge-bags."

"They are not!" said Callum, despite being uncertain of the epithet.

"I had a paper round," Bonk reminisced wistfully.

"Just wait here," said Dogger. "And crouch down a bit in case you can be seen from the car park."

The three moved off.

"Where are you going?" Callum called after them.

"Shut the fuck up!" Logger yelled back.

"We'll just be over there," Dogger waved vaguely at shadows. "On the steps."

Callum nodded. He couldn't see them but he knew where they were; the flight of concrete stairs with a handrail that bisected

4

the embankment and permitted access to the playing field – an alternative to the sliding-down-the-grass-on-your-arse method imposed on Year 7s by bullies.

Within seconds, Callum felt totally alone. He stamped his feet, dreading to think of the state of his shoes, and squatted. He wobbled and feared his trousers might come into contact with the mud. He stood up again, making the concession of hunching his shoulders and bending forward from the waist.

What am I supposed to be watching?

A car trundled along the road beyond the car park but did not stop.

Mum's going to kill me. I should cut across the car park and double back to the bus stop. No. Those three would kill me. Well, Logger certainly would.

I just hope this isn't going to take long.

And then it happened.

2.

Thirty-two inches!

Detective Inspector David Brough was depressed. He looped the tape measure around his naked waist again and checked it a second time. There was no error.

Thirty-two inches.

All his adult life, he had been a snake-hipped twenty-eight. Last year, it had crept up to thirty and now, all of a sudden, another couple of inches had been added to his bulk.

I'm like a whale, he wailed!

Fat, fat bastard. He glowered at his reflection on the wardrobe door. He turned sideways – oh, God! That looked worse! Never mind a muffin-top, I've got the whole fucking cake shop in there.

It turns out middle-age spread is not a medieval margarine.

At my time of life, he reflected – oh, God! I am ANCIENT as well as ENORMOUS! – the metabolism slows. That's science. Biology. He'd read it in a magazine for healthy men. The sobering article had marred his appreciation of the photographs of shirtless hunks with oiled and groomed torsos. Manscaping, they called it. Oscar was into all of that. Oh, God, Oscar – if he sees me all bloated and hideous like this, he'll—

As if summoned, Brough's laptop trilled. An incoming video call. Brough let out a yelp and threw on his dressing gown. He jumped onto the bed and opened the device.

"Hey!" the famous, familiar face grinned at him. Other people all over the world recognised that handsome face from cinema screens, billboards, gossip magazines, and the sides of buses, but to David Brough it was the face of his boyfriend, his largely absentee boyfriend.

6

It was still unfathomably surreal. A Hollywood superstar hooked up with a detective in dreary old Dedley of all places. They had met a couple of years back when Oscar Buzz had come to town to film a big-screen adaptation of some dreadful and defunct soap opera. Since then, the work had been non-stop. It turns out being out in the movie business was no bar to employment after all. Although, the focus was always on Oscar's drop-dead good looks and action-hero physique. The gossip rags were queasy about his sexuality and so they left Brough alone.

Which suits me, Brough considered. What didn't suit him were the extended periods of separation, the forced absences ameliorated only by Skype calls and filthy snapchats.

"You OK, hon?" Oscar Buzz peered at his webcam.

"Yes!" said Brough, a little too quickly.

"Good," said Oscar. "Don't have much time. You ready?"

Somewhere across the globe, in his trailer, Oscar Buzz took off his trousers.

"Um, actually," Brough wrapped his dressing gown tighter. "Can't we just talk? Be a nice change."

"Um…" Oscar looked disappointed. "OK. You talk, I'll get busy."

"No, I mean—"

"Oh, yeah, baby. I love it when you're all assertive."

"Oscar, please!"

"Submissive too. Works for me!"

"Oscar Buzz! Stop wanking and listen to me!"

Oscar paused. "What?"

"Hands where I can see them."

"What?"

"Now!"

"Jeez." Oscar waved his hands at the webcam. "Satisfied? 'Cause I sure ain't."

"It's just that we never talk. There's got to be more to us than long-distance wanking."

"Talk about what?"

"I don't know. Anything. Everything! When am I going to see you?"

"You can see me now."

"I mean in the flesh, not just in the buff."

"I don't know, baby. Schedule's pretty tight. Know what else is pretty tight?" He put a finger in his mouth to wet it.

"Oh, don't! Don't do that!"

Oscar removed the finger and put it somewhere else. His blue eyes widened as it went in.

"I'm terminating this call," Brough warned.

"Oh, come on! I got two minutes tops. At least give me a flash of what I'm missing."

Brough crossed his arms. "Not in the mood."

Oscar glanced away. There was knocking at his trailer door. Brough heard him say "I'll be right out."

"Time's up, baby," Oscar smiled sadly. "I'll call you tonight. Which is tomorrow morning for you, I guess." He kissed his finger – a different finger! – and it grew to fill the screen. "Love you," he said.

The screen went blank.

Brough slammed the laptop shut.

Damn, damn, damn.

He crawled under the covers. He would sleep in his dressing gown; he didn't want to risk glimpsing his ginormous belly again.

***

Logger, Dogger and Bonk watched from behind the privet hedge that separated the Phillipses' front garden from the pavement. A light came on in a first floor window – Callum's parents' bedroom, presumably – and then the hall light. The youths crouched lower as the front door opened and they heard Mrs Phillips let out a cry of alarm and concern, quickly followed by the thud of her son falling face first onto the doormat.

"Callum! Baby!" Mrs Phillips stooped.

"…Mum…" Callum's voice was quiet, distant.

Logger slapped Dogger and signalled with a jerk of his head that they should move on. Dogger repeated the gestures to Bonk. Like a trio of crabs performing a vaudeville song, they crawled along until they were clear of the Phillipses'. Logger stood up straight.

"Another fucking mistake."

"How'd you mean?" said Dogger, also straightening.

"Bringing him here. What if we was seen?"

"We weren't," said Dogger. They strolled briskly away from Callum's street.

"Did you give him his phone back?"

"Yes, I gave him his phone back."

"What a pussy!" Logger marvelled. "Do you remember when you saw it, Dog? Didn't send you all funny, did it?"

"Not like that, no." Dogger's recollection of his own initiation into The Monks had taken on the qualities of a low-budget student horror film in his imagination. "I could tell it was fake from the start."

"Yeah, course you could," Logger was scornful.

"I shit me pants!" declared Bonk. The others came to a halt and stared at him. "I did!" Bonk asserted. "When I saw him floating across that field like that, all glowing, like, I damn near shat myself inside out."

"Unlikely," said Dogger.

"And you can stop fucking crawling now," said Logger.

***

"Hmf?" Detective Sergeant Melanie Miller pawed at her phone, holding it the wrong way up to her ear while simultaneously propping herself up on her elbow. "David?" she half-whispered, half-yawned.

"Oh, good, Miller," Brough's voice blared. "You're still up."

Miller rubbed her eyes with her free hand. "What's up? Is it a murder?"

"Well," said Brough, "It is a death, I suppose."

Miller sat up in bed, suddenly more alert. "Who?"

"The death of my youth," Brough groaned melodramatically.

Not this again, thought Miller. "What was his name, this youth of yours?"

"You're not funny, Miller. I mean my salad days, during which I genuinely did put away a shitload of salad, and yet I've still ballooned up like a – a – well, a balloon."

"You're not a balloon," was Miller's flat reassurance. Honestly. The times she'd had to soothe Brough's ruffled vanity. He was getting worse lately. "Can I go back to sleep now?"

"You mean 'May I," Brough corrected automatically.

"Well, may I?"

"In a bit. Listen, it's not you I want anyway. It's Darren I'm after."

"Well, you can't have him. He's with me now. And most definitely straight, I can tell you."

"There's no accounting for taste, I suppose. I tried his number but it's no longer available or something."

"Um, yes; there was some mix-up with his direct debits."

"So, is he? With you, I mean. As in present, beside you, right this very minute?"

"Yes…"

"Put him on."

"He's asleep."

"Wake him up."

"No!"

"Give him a poke – perhaps I should rephrase that."

"I'll do no such thing. It's late. I'm tired. He's tired. We're all tired. And you – you should be getting your beauty sleep."

Brough let out a squawk and disconnected.

Gotcha! Miller grinned. She snuggled back under the covers. To her right, the broad back of boyfriend Darren Bennett slumbered on. He might not be a Hollywood superstar but he's with me. Here and now.

Smiling smugly, Melanie Miller drifted back to sleep.

3.

"If this is a fucking joke, it isn't fucking funny any fucking more!" Chief Inspector Karen Wheeler stormed around her office – her new office. Superintendent Kevin Ball wisely remained near the exit.

"Karen, please—"

But Wheeler wasn't listening. Ball decided to let her have her rant before trying to get a word in edgewise. 'Let her' – as if anyone 'let' the formidable, foul-mouthed Karen Wheeler do anything.

"It wasn't fucking funny in the first place and it sure as fuck ain't fucking funny now, Kevin."

She seemed to have paused to breathe. Ball opened his mouth but before he could frame a syllable, Wheeler resumed her tirade, her little legs kicking out at anything and everything in her path.

"First we have to sell off Serious because these fucking bastards in government think we can't have nice things, like a decent police force, and so we move into this fucking shithole where there isn't room to fuck a swinging cat, and now you'm telling me we have to up sticks a-fucking-gain and go and work in a fucking supermarket. You can stick that up your bastard arse."

Her shoulders heaving, she sank her fingernails into the back of a chair. Ball saw his chance and seized it.

"This 'shithole' as you so eloquently put it, has served as Dedley's police station for nigh on eighty years."

"So why the fuck are they closing it?"

"It's the latest raft of budget cuts."

"Huh! I remember when Budget Cuts was a cheap hairdresser's on the high street. But a supermarket, Kevin! A fucking supermarket! How am I supposed to run a crack team of detectives in a fucking supermarket? Team briefings on the bacon counter? Set up an incident room in the fruit and veg aisle? Fuck that."

"Karen, Karen. You won't have to. It's only frontline services that will be moved to CostBusters. You and your team can still work here and you won't be disturbed by walk-ins who've had their bicycles nicked or their handbags snatched."

That took the wind out of Wheeler's sails a little. Slightly becalmed, she got her breathing back to normal.

"So why are you telling me all this, Kevin? What's this got to do with me? What's this got to do with Serious?"

Ball paled visibly. "Ah, well, you see…"

"Out with it!"

"To, ah, consolidate your position – your team's position in the town – I mean, this is a prime retail spot; chain stores are queuing up to get this corner – it has been decided that you will oversee our colleagues down the road. At the supermarket."

He flinched and edged closer to the door. Wheeler's eyes bore into him like dentists' drills.

"You want me," she stepped closer to him with every word, "to babysit a bunch of braindead hobby bobbies who can't be trusted to wipe their own arses?"

"Babysitting is the wrong word."

"What then? Nurse-maiding? Zoo-fucking-keeping?"

"Karen, let's keep things in proportion. Perhaps I've come at this from the wrong side. What I should have said was that we need someone of your, ah, stature to ensure that any, um, teething problems that may arise are ironed out."

Wheeler glowered at him with murder in her eyes. "Who agreed? I never agreed."

"The, um, review board. It's the best solution. With a limited purse—"

"Oh, blow it out your arse, Kevin. Don't bend me over a barrel, shaft me dry and tell me you can't afford to spit on it first."

Ball turned red. "I am sorry; it's the way of the world, Karen. This government—"

"Can kiss my arse." Deflated, Wheeler sat at her desk. She opened a folder. "These the details?"

"Yes. I knew you'd see reason."

"Fuck off."

***

In an unprecedented move on his part, Logger was one of the first to turn up for school that morning. Rather than sloping across the field (via the gap in the railings) long after Assembly had started, he was there, not exactly bright of eye and bushy of tail, waiting anxiously for the caretaker to unlock the gates. He scoured the road in both directions, a leafy avenue of rather big houses, watching every approaching person and vehicle with keen interest.

He reminded himself the specky twat used the bus. What time did that pull in? The nearest stop was a couple of streets away – should Logger linger there instead? He wasn't sure which bus exactly. The only way to be certain was to wait at the main entrance.

"Lawrence?" Mr Wazley paused in his briefcase swinging to examine the youth who had arrived at school before he did. "Well, well. This is encouraging, I must say. Or—" his eyes narrowed mischievously, "are you still here from last night's detention?"

Logger curled his lip. Mr Wazley chuckled and headed to Reception, a hallowed entrance reserved for Staff and Visitors only.

"Sarky twat," Logger muttered when the teacher was well out of earshot. He returned his attention to the street. More and more kids were arriving, many of them congregating in groups, making it increasingly difficult for Logger to have a clear view. He shoved a couple of Year 7s aside as a car pulled up onto the yellow zigzags at the kerb. The passenger door opened and a smart shoe, newly polished, touched the tarmac, but Callum Phillips's mother wasn't ready to let her son go yet. Above the soothing strains of Classic FM that wafted from the open door, Logger heard the strident admonitions of Mrs Phillips.

"Look lively, Callum., for pity's sake. You've been in a proper doze since you got in last night. Do you want me to walk you in? I could go in and have a word with that head teacher. Keeping you here until all hours, sending you home in that state. Anyone would think you'd been mud-wrestling, the state of your shoes."

"Mum…" said Callum. It was a warning and a plea. He had spotted Logger, who was approaching.

"Is it a bully, Callum? Did he throw you down that slope?"

"No!" Callum cried. He tried to get out but forgot he was still wearing his seatbelt. His mother released him and he sprang forward into Logger's chest. Logger righted him and, turning on an uncharacteristic smile, waved cheerily to Mrs Phillips until she drove away. The smile dropped from his lips and he squeezed Callum's elbow and steered him away from the gates.

"But – Registration—" Callum pointed wildly at the building.

"Bollocks to it," said Logger. "You and me am going to have a nice chat."

***

"It's all quiet on the West Midlands front," Wheeler seemed unhappy to announce to the Serious Crimes team, who assembled for a briefing. "Fucking dead as a dodo's fucking doorknob."

Detective Inspector Harry Henry blinked and pushed his loose-fitting spectacles back up the bridge of his nose. "Don't you mean 'doornail', Chief?"

The correction earned him a glare from the diminutive chief inspector.

"Dead as a doornail's fucking doorknob then," she spat, "as if that makes any fucking sense."

Detective Inspector Benny Stevens let out a laugh. He wiped drops of tea from his porn-star moustache. "Anybody'd think you want folk to murder each other, Boss."

Wheeler rounded on him. "Of course I fucking don't. Although it would give you lot something to do. Honestly, here we am, facing another round of budget cuts – it's like *they* want people to get away with murder. A big, juicy case right about now would make it easier to justify all our jobs. As it is, we'm all going to take on extra duties to keep us busy."

Detective Constable Jason Pattimore raised his hand. He waited for Wheeler's nod before posing his question. "What sort of extra duties, Boss?"

"Ah, Jason, I'm glad you asked. You and Stevens am going into schools. Give them the old say-fuck-off-to-drugs bit. Chuck in some road safety while you'm at it."

Pattimore nodded and made notes.

"Fuck sake," Stevens complained. "Do we have to?"

Wheeler answered him with a humourless display of her teeth. She turned to Brough and Miller.

"David, Melanie, it's the posh estates for you. Crime prevention. Give your advice on window locks and keeping sheds secure, all that bollocks."

"Um, why the posh estates?" Miller ventured to ask.

"Because," said Brough, "they're the ones with stuff worth nicking."

"Oh," Miller shrank back, blushing at her own foolishness.

"Not fair!" Stevens pointed an accusing finger. "Why should they get the cushy job and me and Jase get thrown to the teenage shitheads."

"Just lucky, I guess," said Wheeler.

"Um…" Harry Henry raised a tentative hand. "What about me, Chief?"

"What about you?"

"What are my extra duties?" He was on the edge of his seat.

"Filing."

"Come again?"

"There's still a shitload of boxes of shit from the Serious building, God rest its soul. Need sorting out. You're the man for that job."

"Sweet!" Harry Henry's face lit up. He even rubbed his hands in gleeful anticipation.

"Hang about," Stevens raised another objection. "How come he gets to sort through paperwork while me and Jase—"

Wheeler cut him off. "Because you're practically fucking illiterate. Now, if there's nothing else," she prepared to jerk her thumb toward the exit.

"Hold up," Stevens got to his feet. He towered over Wheeler – but then, most people did. "What's your extra duties, if it ain't a rude question?"

Wheeler would not be cowed. "It is a rude fucking question. If you must know, I'm off to Costbosters to knock a couple of PCSO heads together. Perhaps I could warm up with you?"

Stevens backed off, his eyes averted.

"Good," said Wheeler. Her thumb was primed. She used it. "Now, fuck off."

***

With the rest of the school ensconced in Assembly or Form Period, Logger skulked around the building and across the field to intercept Dogger and Bonk when they arrived through the fence. With his hood up, he would be unidentifiable from a distance but Logger was not entirely stupid; he had a note in his pocket excusing him for a dental appointment should he be intercepted by a member of staff.

"All right, Log?" Dogger was amazed. Ordinarily, it was he and Bonk who were kept waiting for Logger. "What's going on?"

Logger's eyes shifted from side to side. He gestured toward the bushes. "Got any fags, Bonk? I bloody need one."

Bonk produced a single cigarette from somewhere on his person. Dogger provided the lighter – it belonged to Bonk but he could not be trusted with flammable items. Logger received the offerings with curt nods of gratitude. He lit the cigarette and took a long, restorative drag. The others watched and waited.

"I have just had a very interesting conversation with that specky wanker."

"Who?" said Bonk.

"He means Callum. From last night," Dogger translated but Bonk seemed none the wiser.

"Told me all about last night, he did." Logger stared directly at Dogger, his gaze burning as bright as his cigarette end. "Do you know if he has a history of mental health problems?"

Dogger's blank look indicated that he knew nothing of the sort.

"He told me," Logger's voice was constricted more from emotion than the intake of smoke and chemicals. "He told me what he sid last night changed his life. I asked him to tell me about it in detail, like, and he only fucking did." Logger's lip was quivering, the cigarette sticking to it, forgotten.

"He said it came from over there, faint at first, and shapeless but as it drew nearer it took on the shape of a man, a man in a hooded robe with an empty space where his face should be. And he said even though it had no face, he could tell it was looking right at him, and it pointed at him and all, even though it looked like there was no hand sticking out of the end of the sleeve. It pointed right at him. And then – *whoosh*! – it was gone."

Dogger and Bonk were speechless and open-mouthed. They looked across the field, so everyday and harmless-looking in the cold light of morning, and pictured the scene. Over there was the row of bushes where they'd told the King of Nerds to crouch.

"So, he saw it then," Dogger shrugged. "We've all sid it."

But Logger was shaking his head. "Not like this we didn't."

"So, the boss has improved his special effects budget."

"That's just it." Logger took out his phone and held it at arm's length so Dogger could read the screen. "Got that last night before I went to sleep. Only I didn't get no sleep after that, did I?"

Dogger squinted at the text message, frowning because Logger's hand was shaking considerably. Dogger met Logger's gaze. Together their heads turned to look out across the field.

"Fucking hell," they said in unison.

"Here, Log," said Bonk. "You going to finish that fag or what?"

***

Brough tapped his foot impatiently while he waited for Miller to come out of the Ladies. She always seemed to take bloody ages. It's different for women, he supposed. A man can just slide down a zipper or undo a few buttons. With women it was more complicated – and Miller was wearing tights.

He reminded himself not to let his impatience show; he needed to keep Miller sweet enough to grant him a favour.

At long last, she emerged with her hair brushed and a fresh coat of lippy applied. No bloody wonder she takes so long, thought Brough. Every trip to the lav is like a bloody visit to a spa. He noted with disdain a square of toilet paper dragging under her heel but refrained from mentioning it.

"Miller…" he began as they walked to her car. "*Mel…*"

"What?" She fished in her capacious bag for her keys. Why she couldn't keep them in her pocket, Brough would never know. The workings of the female mind (and body too) were as unknowable to Brough as the dark side of the moon.

"Your Darren…"

"What about him?"

"Has he got any gaps?"

"How'd you mean? In his teeth?"

"Any spaces. If he has, I'd like to fill one."

"I'm not sure I like the sound of this. A-ha!" She pulled her fist from her bag in triumph. She unlocked the car and got in, then reached across to unlock the passenger door.

"So, has he?" said Brough, fastening his seatbelt.

"Has he what?"

"Any spaces. In his schedule."

"What are you talking about?"

"He's a personal trainer, isn't he? I'd like to book some sessions with him."

"I bet you would."

"Not like that. So, has he?"

"I don't know, do I?"

"Will you ask him?"

"Ask him yourself."

"I can't, can I?"

"Why not?"

"His phone's out of commission, isn't it? That 'mix-up'?"

"Oh, no; I sorted that." Miller started the engine.

"I'll phone him later then."

"Suit yourself."

They drove out of the town centre and up a hill to the well-to-do Hemlock estate.

"Um, Miller…"

"If you want to phone him, phone him. I'm not his keeper."

"I will. But it's not that. The box of crime prevention leaflets."

"Don't tell me they've been nicked. I thought you had them."

"I did. I sort of left them on the roof of your car."

Miller looked in the rear-view mirror. Sure enough, a host of printed material was swarming in their wake. "Shit!" She pulled over.

"Oops," said Brough. He unbuckled and got out. Miller watched his reflection jumping around like a cat swatting butterflies. Usually she would be tickled by such a sight. But not this time. She chewed her lower lip, ruining its recently applied coat.

Where's your head at, David? Too caught up in your bloody vanity to keep your mind on the job.

It was fortunate they had nothing more serious than a few crime prevention visits to make.

***

"Come on, then." Pattimore unfastened his seatbelt. Stevens was still gripping the steering wheel of his Ford Capri, even though they had arrived at the school's car park minutes ago. Pattimore let out a laugh of amazement. "Are you scared? You are! You're scared."

"Get fucked," snarled Stevens. "I just don't like schools, that's all. Never have, never will."

"Aw," Pattimore teased. "Have a hard time, did you? Did those nasty big boys flush Benny's head down the bog?"

"Piss off. I was the nasty big boy."

"Somehow I believe that. Now, are you coming in or are you going to wait in the car like a neglected doggy? I can wind the window down a bit if you are."

"I'm not."

"Not what?"

"Not fucking scared."

"If you say so."

"I'll show you who's scared." Stevens snatched the key from the ignition and climbed out of the car. He looked at the oblong building of concrete and glass before him. "It hasn't changed a bit," he observed, his moustache quivering.

"What?" said Pattimore. "You went here? You went to Hangham High?"

"Yup. It was a shithole then and it's a shithole now."

"Looks all right to me. Bit Brutalist but that's all the rage these days. Back in fashion."

"Mate, it was the brutallest time of my life."

"That's not what I meant. You see, there's this school—"

"I can see it."

"No, this school of architecture—"

"Christ! I don't want to hear it. How long's it been since you broke up with Brough? It was him who filled your head with bollocks."

Pattimore grinned. "Once or twice, yes."

Stevens was aghast. "Hoi! I don't want to hear that neither. This is a school. You can't be gay here."

"Who says?"

"It's the law."

"Since when?"

"I don't bloody know."

"You're ridiculous."

"I'm only looking out for you, that's all. I've got your back."

"Wahey!"

"That's exactly the kind of thing I'm on about. Just keep your head down."

"Ha!"

"I'm serious, Jase. A place like this can be hard for a – well, a – somebody like you."

Pattimore's incredulity gave way to a different emotion. "I'm touched."

"Not by me you won't be. Bring that box off the back seat. I'll do the talking."

Stevens marched away. Pattimore called him back. "Where are you going?"

"Inside!"

"Reception's around the front. You are allowed in the main entrance now, you know."

Stevens blinked. "Oh, yeah."

***

Wheeler parked beneath the supermarket; there was nothing unusual in that. In fact, everyone was doing it. The massive shop stood over a car park like a colossal mother hen guarding her eggs. A stairless escalator carried her to the shop floor, a harshly-lit hangar crammed with goods from all around the globe. If you could name it, you could find it under this roof. Or its gluten-free equivalent.

Wheeler was blind to the smorgasbord of international fare on offer. She headed directly to a corner of the building where a café was situated, an in-store branch of *Queequeg's*, rubbing elbows with a key-cutting stall, a dry cleaner's, and a passport photography service. In front of all of these, a trestle table had been set up and an A4 sheet of paper had been taped forlornly to it, advertising 'Deldey Pollice'. A couple of garden chairs were behind the table, both of them devoid of backsides.

"Arseholes!" Wheeler growled. She cast a murderous look around. You didn't have to be a chief inspector at the helm of a crack squad of detectives to figure out where the good-for-nothing hobby bobbies had sloped off to.

The coffee bar was also serving doughnuts.

Sure enough, the bright lemon yellow of the PCSOs' tabards was easily discernible among the café's brown and cream furnishings. The arseholes she sought were in a booth, laughing through gobfuls of fat and sugar. Wheeler's blood began to percolate. She tapped her foot but managed to refrain from flipping the table over.

Instead, she pulled out one of the chairs and sat. It was a low seat and not a good fit. Her chin could easily rest on the table top.

She waited. Like a spider, she waited.

A young man approached, wearing the navy blue jersey of the in-store security. His shoulders were adorned with fake leather epaulettes and his peaked cap bore the CB monogram that all of the supermarket's employees were obliged to sport. A name tag revealed him to be Charlie West. Wheeler was singularly unimpressed.

"Yo cor sit there, bab," Charlie West shook his head. "That's for the coppers. If they catch you sitting there, yo'll be for it."

"Fuck off," said Wheeler.

The security guard was taken aback. "Now, now, chicken; there's no need for that. Is your carer around?"

Wheeler got to her feet. Enough of her was visible now for Charlie West to see her serge uniform with its silver buttons and other marks of rank.

"I'm sorry, sir – er – ma'm," he stammered. "I didn't realise."

"Remember when I told you to fuck off."

Charlie West scrambled away. Wheeler smirked. She ran a hand over her salt-and-pepper crew cut, pleased that she had not lost her touch.

"Aye, aye," said a voice. The PCSOs were on their way back. "What's all this then? Fancy dress?"

"Aren't you a bit old for dressing-up, love? What's the matter? They run out of Cinderella frocks in your size?"

Their laughter stopped gurgling like a swiftly plugged sink when Chief Inspector Wheeler turned the full force of her Rottweiler scowl in their direction.

"Hello, wankers." She smiled like an ingratiating crocodile. "Sit the fuck down and explain your-fucking-selves."

4.

During break, the Monks reconvened on the concrete stairs that led to the field. Lesser mortals would rather scramble up or down the grassy embankment rather than pay the toll – with dinner money largely involving electronic transactions in this digital age, the Monks extracted payment of a different kind in the form of doling out dead arms and legs to those who wished to pass.

But on this occasion, their minds had another focus and several bold Year 8 boys slipped by unmarked and unpunched.

"It's really weird," Dogger was repeating, "All through Maths he just sat there when, usually, he's rattling off sums and equations like nobody's business. But he just sat there, staring at nothing. Even the teacher noticed. Well, she was bound to, wasn't she? And she asks him if everything's all right and he just carries on staring like he's looking right through her and there's a little smile at the corner of his mouth, like he knows a secret, and eventually she gives up and says as long as he does them for homework she'll let him off, and she laughs and says it'll give the rest of us chance to catch up."

"Fuck me," said Logger.

"Who are we talking about?" said Bonk. "Oh, hello, Callum!"

The other two jumped; they had not seen the subject of their discussion approach. Callum Phillips grinned at them from under the hood of his new top.

"Well met, fellows!" he slapped Bonk on the back. What was even more astonishing than this was Bonk didn't appear to mind. Logger and Dogger exchanged glances of disbelief.

Callum surveyed the field with evident disdain. "This place is for kids and arseholes," he declared. "And I'm neither of those. Are you?"

"No fucking way!" Logger asserted.

"Not me!" Dogger asserted.

"Who's he calling a kid?" Bonk asked.

"I say we clear off," Callum stretched as though stirring himself from terminal boredom. "Go somewhere else."

The bell announced the end of break. Kids began to shuffle toward the entrances with a total lack of enthusiasm.

"What, now?" said Dogger.

"No, Bastille Day! Of course now!" snapped Callum.

"Where to?" Logger narrowed his eyes.

Callum returned Logger's hard stare. "Into town," he shrugged. "Or somewhere."

"Like where?"

"We can improvise."

"Ooh!" Bonk perked up. "Like in Drama? We're in a bus stop and one of us is a space alien."

Callum was already moving off, striding toward the fence with its well-used gap. He felt energised. Confident. And all it had taken was reeling off some bullshit about seeing the ghost of some old monk that was said to haunt the playing field. He'd read about it and those three suckers had fallen for it without question.

The founding members of the Monks looked at each other. Behind them lay the prospect of Double Geography. Ahead was the prospect of adventure.

"Cal! Wait up!" Dogger loped after the new recruit.

"Come on then, Bonk," Logger heaved his shoulders. "Geography's a load of wank anyway."

Bonk frowned in confusion as he followed the others. "Don't you like wanking then, Log?"

***

Beatrice Mooney, head of Priory High, was going to be late for her meeting. Traffic through Dedley was always a nightmare; the town could do with a ring road, she reflected – and not for the first time. Perhaps she should bring up the matter during her meeting… No, not this time. She needed to be sure what she wanted was safely in the bag before she ruffled any more feathers.

The car behind hers sounded its horn, rousing her from her ring road reverie. She sent the driver a curt snarl via the rear-view mirror and moved on. A few yards later, she came to another standstill.

Great. Just bloody great. How is it going to look if I can't even show up on time? How can I hope to persuade local businessmen to invest millions?

The horn sounded again.

Beatrice Mooney scowled. She caught her own eye. Her mascara could do with a brush-up before the meeting. It wouldn't do to turn up late and looking like a raccoon who'd been watching chick flicks.

She was approaching the broad intersection that linked the town to Tipton to the left, Smethwick straight ahead and also, seven or eight miles to the right, Birmingham, city of her birth. Beatrice Mooney's voice betrayed no hint of her native accent – not unless she'd had more than a couple of Malibu-and-cokes.

She waited at the lights, tapping her fingers on the rim of the steering wheel not quite in time with the radio. At her left was the humungous supermarket that was leaching business out of the town centre shops. It was a shame, really. But, oh well, times change.

She resolved to tamp down her objection to the supermarket and attempt to forget it forever. One of the men she was due to meet was the CEO of *CostBusters*. Dennis – something. Shit. I'd better bone up on my notes while I'm touching up my mascara.

More angry honking. From several cars this time.

Four hooded youths were ambling across the carriageway with no apparent respect for the Green Cross Code. Bloody kids. Beatrice Mooney's slightly smudged eyes followed the miscreants as they passed in front of her bonnet on their way to the supermarket. With their jackets zipped to their chins and their hoods shading their faces she couldn't tell if they were Priory High kids or not. Had the lights remained red, she would have wound a window down and challenged them about not being in school – any school. But amber changed to green and rather than risk the wrath of that wanker behind, she continued her journey, taking a right toward Birmingham.

Forget it, she told herself. Those little shits are most probably from Hangham High.

***

"They'm out as well." Miller trudged from the front door of the latest house she'd tried. Brough was waiting at the end of the path, busy with his smartphone.

"Of course they're out, Miller. How do you think they can afford houses like this?"

"I suppose. How are we supposed to dispense crime prevention advice if nobody's bloody in?"

"You left the appointment card."

"I did."

"I know you did. I can see it protruding from the letterbox. Honestly, Miller." Brough strode up the path and pushed the leaflet through until it dropped out of sight on the other side of the door. "Post sticking out is a sure sign no one's home. You might as well send out invitations to every burglar in Dedley."

Miller scowled.

"So, you'd better go back along the street and make sure there's nothing else poking out."

Disgruntled, Miller stomped back the way they had come. She turned, thinking she'd show him something else poking out but Brough was preoccupied with his phone again and so the brief appearance of Miller's tongue went unnoticed.

When she returned, Brough held up his hand in that imperious manner people have when they're making a call. Miller had to wait until he'd finished. The call seemed to consist almost entirely of laughter. At long last, he disconnected and pocketed the device.

"Oscar?" ventured Miller.

"No. If you must know, Miller, it was your Darren."

"Why were you phoning my Darren?" Miller knew why; what she really wanted to know was why were they both laughing so much.

"I said I'd phone him. So I did."

Miller pouted.

"Oh, don't get into a strop, Miller. It was purely a business call." "Huh."

"I've booked your Darren for some training sessions in the park. He was glad of it. The business, I mean."

Miller grunted. Ever since Darren had been laid off from the leisure centre – thanks to more swingeing cuts to the council budget – and had gone freelance, money was tight. Miller supposed she ought to be grateful to Brough for not opting for Dedley's gay gym, *The Muscle Hustle*. And it wasn't as if she didn't trust Darren. He was a hundred per cent straight, she was sure of it. And it wasn't as if she didn't trust Brough, who had integrity and was hooked up with one of the hottest film stars on the planet. It was just – well – when two people you know from different contexts get together and you're not there – well – you're bound to feel a bit insecure, aren't you? They're bound to talk about you, aren't they? You're their common ground.

"We're having our first session later," added Brough as they headed back to Miller's car. "He said he'll have me sweating in seconds and every inch of me groaning in agony in half an hour."

Not helping, thought Miller.

***

29

To say that Stevens's presentation had gone badly would be an understatement, like saying the Titanic had had one or two teething problems. Pattimore stood, arms folded, in the car park while Stevens backed out of the door, shedding paraphernalia from the box he was cradling and hurling invective, even when the door had closed.

"Yeah, well, you can stick your Health and Safety up your arse!" he jeered. He pressed the box against Pattimore's chest. The detective constable was forced to take it or drop the lot, and he would rather not prolong their visit to Hangham High by another second. In fact, he would rather it had never happened at all.

Stevens strode briskly to his Capri, swearing through his moustache. "Fucking idiots! You try to tell them something that will save their shitty lives."

"You're not supposed to show them how to shoot up."

The remark earned Pattimore a steely-eyed glare. Stevens yanked open the door, got in and started the engine. Pattimore had to scramble to get in the passenger side in order to avoid being left behind. Stevens spun the wheels and then peeled out, tyres screeching, before Pattimore had chance to buckle himself in.

Out in Dedley traffic, Stevens was forced to slow down and calm down. "A misunderstanding," he growled. "A fucking misunderstanding. All I said was if you'm going to inject smack, make sure there's no air bubbles in the syringe. And they try to tell *me* about Health and fucking Safety!" He laughed once, a bitter, hollow sound.

"Ben, you tied a length of rubber tubing around a kid's arm."

"He volunteered! He was well up for it."

"His hand was turning blue!"

"I couldn't find a vein, could I? Fat bastard. There's child obesity for you right there."

"I think the point is we're supposed to deter them from using drugs, not show them how to do it."

"I did! I bloody did! I said, didn't I, don't piss around with all this shit. Booze is cheaper and widely available."

"That didn't help."

"It was a *joke*, for fuck's sake. Do you honestly think any of those Year 7s could get served? Not even at the dodgiest off-licence. They'd get laughed right out of *Cigs, Figs and Wigs*."

"That's not the point."

"And I hadn't even made a start on the glue-sniffing."

"Thank God for that! It was supposed to be Road Safety with the Year 7s and Drug Awareness with Year 10. I kept trying to signal to you from the back."

"Did you? I thought you were just arsing about, trying to put me off. Threatening to cut my throat; I don't bloody know, do I?"

"Well, I just hope that deputy head doesn't complain to Wheeler."

Stevens paled and wailed. "Fuck me." He turned the car around. "Pub?" he suggested."

"Pub," Pattimore sighed.

* * *

"So, let me get this straight," Wheeler wiped latte foam from her upper lip. "You have to sit in the café because the Wi-Fi signal's better in here."

Across the booth, the PCSOs nodded rapidly. One of them pushed a plate piled high with doughnuts closer to the chief inspector.

"For your tablet?"

"Yes." The other PCSO held up the device in question, as though modelling a prize in a game show.

"And you expect me to swallow that?"

The PCSOs smiles faltered. They exchanged nervous looks. Wheeler laughed.

"I'm only pulling your penises, lads. For fuck's sake! Tablet, swallow it. Don't you fucking get it?"

The PCSOs laughed, more from fear than amusement.

As part of an initiative to cut down on paperwork as much as expenditure, the PCSOs had been issued with a single tablet between them.

"It's a paperless office," said the first PCSO.

"It's a fucking officeless office," Wheeler retorted. "But I'm not convinced feeding your faces in here all day conveys the right image."

"Oh, it ain't all day," they were keen to point out. "We only get refreshments when it's our breaks."

"On the house!" the other added, smugly.

Wheeler stared at her milky coffee. "So, this isn't paid for?"

"No!" the PCSOs laughed.

"Ain't it brilliant?"

Wheeler narrowed her eyes. "So, you'm telling me you'm accepting bribes from this establishment."

The PCSOs gaped.

Wheeler chuckled. She took a slurp of her coffee. "More penis-pulling, lads. I suppose having you two bruisers in here means they don't have trouble with fuckwits."

The PCSOs nodded rapidly. "It's a kind of partnership, you might say."

"Like an outreach whatsit type of thing."

Wheeler's expression soured. "Oh, no. Don't you start spouting that bollocks. I might as well go and talk to Superintendent Ball."

The PCSOs relaxed – a little – pleased to hear this indiscreet remark.

"And have you had much cause to use it? Your fucking tablet, I mean. Many enquiries from the public?"

"Not a one."

"Nobody knows we'm here."

They did their best to look downcast.

"Hmm," said Wheeler, making a mental note. "Names? What are your names? I can't go on calling you Prick One and Prick Two."

"Um," said the first. "My name's Hobley. Robert Hobley."

"Robert Hobley…" Wheeler repeated, fixing the name and the face in her memory.

"But you can call me Bobby."

Wheeler baulked. "The fuck I will. Bobby Hobley the hobby bobby! It's got to be a fucking joke."

"It ain't!"

"Now who's pulling whose penis?"

"I—"

Bobby Hobley put his hands on the table in full view. Wheeler turned to the other officer who looked decidedly sweatier than a moment ago. "Don't tell me; you'm called something saft as well. Like, I don't know, fucking Pat Rolcar, or something."

"Er – no."

"I'm fucking tickled to hear it. Well?"

"I am, thank you."

"Jesus wept. Your name, sunshine?"

"Um…"

"Come on. Let's be fucking having it."

"It's – er – it's…" the poor man couldn't meet the chief inspector's gaze – but then, few can. "It's Wren."

"Wren. Good."

"Simon Wren."

"Good."

"Si for short."

Simon Wren cringed, waiting for the penny to drop. Wheeler's eyes bored into him. She blinked.

"Fuck off," she said.

At that point, store security guard Charlie West approached. "Um…"

Wheeler smiled sweetly. "Yes, chicken?"

"If we could have a bit of help? Only there's some trouble. Some kids running around."

Wheeler got to her feet. "This is more fucking like it. Lay on, Macduff."

"No, it's West. Charlie West."

"Whatever. Come on, Prick One, Prick Two. Off your arseholes. Time to burn off that fucking biscotti."

5.

Brough and Miller separated for lunch. She dropped him at his flat where he changed into an expensive tracksuit and top-of-the-range trainers. A spot of physical exertion will perk me right up, he thought, carrying out a few stretches to warm up. Handing out fucking crime prevention leaflets was beneath him, he felt. The sooner someone murdered someone in this town the better.

The intercom buzzed. Brough pressed a button.

"It's me," said the voice of Darren Bennett.

"I'll be right down."

Enjoy your lonely cheese and onion roll, Miller, Brough smirked as he jogged down the stairs. I'm going to feast my eyes on your boyfriend's buns.

Well, sneaking the occasional glance wouldn't hurt, would it?

"How do," said Darren. His eyes travelled up and down Brough's attire. "Nice threads."

Brough looked at Darren's own threadbare and misshapen jogging bottoms and wished he could return the compliment. "It's what's inside that counts," he said. He blushed.

"Come on then," Darren was already loping off down the street. "I'm going to work you so hard."

"Ha!" Brough ran leisurely behind, enjoying the view. It was like two basketballs in a sack. "Don't let Mel hear you say things like that."

***

"Well, we can't keep waiting forever." Dennis Lord strode around the rather beige conference room on the ground floor of the Apex Hotel, near Junction 2 of the M5. A featureless place, surrounded by industrial parks and drive-through burger bars. "You can't make a fortune waiting around for other people to show up. And, as you may be aware, this ain't my only project. I do have other irons in the pie."

Beatrice Mooney blushed beneath her foundation, detecting a reference to her own tardiness. She had arrived, immaculate but flustered, only twenty minutes after she was expected, certain she had incurred at least two speeding fines along the way, only to be told by the CEO of *CostBusters* that it was a lady's prerogative and she wasn't to worry her pretty little head about it.

And now the sexist pig was bemoaning the no-show of the fourth member of the quartet. "Have you phoned him, Barry?"

Barry Norwood, deputy leader of Dedley Council, waved his mobile in the air. His ear was hot from holding the device to it for the past half hour. "I've phoned him, Dennis. I've phoned him repeatedly. It's just ringing out."

"Perhaps that means he's on his way," Beatrice offered. "You know the traffic is bad. Perhaps he can't answer while he's driving."

Dennis Lord's lip curled in a surly manner. "He should get a fucking long tooth."

"Bluetooth," offered Barry.

"A fucking headset. I'll send him one over from my customer care centre. You can answer the phone anywhere with one of them. Hands free. It don't matter what you'm doing. I told them, down the call centre, I told them there's no more need for toilet breaks, they can still field calls when they'm on the shitter."

He laughed. "It was only a joke. At the time, like. But now I'm thinking..." he shook his head. "Have you left him a message, Barry?"

"I've left him a message, Dennis. I've left him no end of messages."

"Well, like I said, we can't go on waiting here forever. I say we make a start. The sooner we finish the sooner we can fuck off. I've got nine holes waiting for me, if you know what I mean."

"Golf?" said Beatrice Mooney.

"No. Triplets."

"Right, then!" Barry Norwood clapped his hands together. "In Paul's absence, I can say, and I don't think he'd be averse to me saying it, that he's not willing to increase his stake. Not without some substantial and significant changes being made. Or assurances thereof."

"Changes?" Dennis Lord behaved as if he'd never heard the word. "What bloody changes is he on about?"

"Well – and don't shoot the messenger here, Dennis – principally the name."

"He can fuck off," Dennis sat back and crossed his arms. "If he was here, I'd tell him to his face he can fuck off again."

"I'm only saying what he emailed me."

"Bah! What's wrong with the name any road?"

"Do you mean," Beatrice arched a perfect eyebrow, "*CostBusters Academy*?"

"Good name is that."

"It is a bit on the nose," Beatrice continued. "And I thought it had been agreed – that we'd all agreed – the name is to be truncated to C. B. Academy. Although, I am a bit concerned about two thousand children with badges on their blazers saying C.B.A. It hardly gives the right impression."

"Balls," said Dennis Lord. "I see what he's doing. Bloody Paul. He knows he can't get his way with the name. So he's chucked his babby out the pram."

"Dummy, surely?" queried Beatrice.

"What?"

"He's thrown his dummy from his pram. Not his baby."

"Same difference, love."

"Now," Barry Norwood interjected. "Let's not get caught up in semantics."

"Ha!" Dennis laughed. "I fully intend to. Later on. After this.

With the triplets. Get caught up in some antics! Do you get it?"

Beatrice Mooney smiled thinly. Odious man! What am I doing, letting him within coo-ee of my school?

Oh, yes.

She remembered the generous augmentation of her savings account.

"Look, Dennis; the point is Paul's not in your league. None of our other sponsors is. But unless they feel they hold some sway, they'll pull out – and please don't twist my words to another unseemly reference to your afternoon's entertainment."

"How'd you mean?"

"Never mind."

"Listen, sugar. This is how it is. I'm stumping up the most moolah so I get to say what's what regarding the fabric of the building. Paul Barker and the rest of them can stamp their bloody logos on the other stuff. The exercise books, for example – do kids still use them? – even the fabric of the fucking curtains, I don't give a flying shit. I'll leave it to your capable hands to sort out the finer details. On with business. Cop a load of this."

He unrolled a huge sheet of paper, an architect's drawing of the proposed new academy.

"One or two tweaks – as the bishop said to the topless actress – and something new. See if you can spot it."

Barry and Beatrice pored over the drawing as though it was a treasure map. Beatrice saw it first.

"Oh, no," she paled.

"Oh, yes!"

"Is that what I think it is?"

"I don't know; I'm not a bastard mind-reader, am I, love?"

"What are we looking at?" blinked Barry.

"I'm not having it!" Beatrice cried.

"Then buy a vibrator," said Dennis.

"I won't allow it! A supermarket on site!"

"Calm your tits, Bea. It's a *mini-mart*, that's all. That's the thing I miss most about school. The tuck shop. So here's one writ big. To be manned – well, boyed and girled – by the kids themselves. It's a learning opportunity, ain't it?"

"It says twenty-four hour opening."

"Nothing wrong with your eyesight."

"Mr Lord, are you suggesting the students open the shop around the clock? You are! You're – you're going to allow the public in, aren't you? Onto school grounds!"

Dennis Lord's smile dropped. "I've got overheads. Place like this won't pay for itself if we only open at playtime. I don't expect you to appreciate the retail sector, love."

"Because I'm a woman?"

"Don't do yourself down, love. I mean because you're an academic. An educator. And, as an educator, you must see what a marvellous opportunity it is for your customers – I mean the kids – to prepare them for the world of work."

"Working for you, you mean."

"Way of the world, flower. Tell you what: I'll up the ante. Another ten per cent. Another *personal* ten per cent." He winked and tapped the side of his nose.

"All right," Beatrice Mooney relented. "You can have your little shop."

"Excellent!" said Barry Norwood. "Those lucky children!"

"That's my girl," grinned Dennis Lord. "Now be a darling and pour me another coffee."

***

"The pricks!"

"Yes, ma'm!" PCSOs Hobley and Wren stood to attention.

"Not you two," Wheeler rolled her eyes. "This lot." She jerked her thumb at the bank of CCTV monitors. They were watching playback of the rampage of the gang of four hooded youths. The louts worked with co-ordination, pushing each other in shopping trolleys into displays, hurling cartons of milk like Molotov cocktails to keep all who might approach and challenge them at bay, duelling with French loaves and cucumbers, and generally wreaking havoc and leaving devastation in their wake.

Charlie West could barely bring himself to watch. He clapped a hand to his face and took tentative peeks through his fingers, wincing as every item hit the floor.

"That's you, look, Charlie!" Si Wren chuckled. "Oops, mind you don't slip on those eggs. Oh! Down he goes."

"Wahey!" Bobby Hobley joined in.

"Pricks," muttered Wheeler.

"Ain't they just," Si Wren agreed.

"Not them; you two. Give me strength."

On a monitor, the PCSOs bumbled into frame, getting in each other's way and slapping each other.

"It's like the fucking Keystone Kops after budget cuts," Wheeler growled.

The PCSOs moved to another screen, shown from a different angle, slipping and sliding through spilled milk and burst packets of flour and crisps. At the end of the aisle, one of the youths was standing, his back to them. The hobby bobbies nudged each other. They each selected a packet of flour from the shelves and launched them at the vandal. Who ducked down at the last second. The bags of flour hit Chief Inspector Wheeler in the face, knocking her on her arse. The screen filled with flour like a self-raising mushroom cloud.

"Oops," muttered Bobby Hobley, chewing his thumb in order to suppress his giggles.

Just as Charlie West was about to make a citizen's arrest by grabbing one of the hoods, the PCSOs, in their flight from Wheeler, skidded into him, bringing him down on top of themselves. Three pairs of feet and legs sprang up along the bottom of the screen while, on another monitor, the four hoodlums exchanged congratulatory high-fives and skedaddled from the building.

"What an utter fucking shambles!" Wheeler switched the monitors back to 'live'. Staff cleaning up the fucking shambles bobbed in and out of view.

"I almost had him," Charlie West hit his forehead with the heel of his hand.

"Did you see his face?" Wheeler urged. "Could you identify him if you saw him again?"

Charlie West answered no to both questions. In doing so, Charlie West lied to the police.

Twice.

***

Brough took a hefty swig from his water bottle and wiped sweat from his forehead with the back of his hand.

"I have to say," Darren Bennett panted between words, "I didn't think you'd be able to keep it up."

"Why?" Brough bristled. "Because I'm so very old?"

"Nah, what are you? Thirty-three, thirty-four."

"I like you," grinned Brough, neglecting to correct him. "Then you think I'm fat? Out of shape?"

"No, no! You're pretty trim, you know. What I've seen." Darren drank from his own water bottle and licked his lips. Brough forced himself to look away from the sweat-stained T-shirt that was clinging to Darren's pectorals. The instructor had been an incorrigible flirt ever since Brough and Miller had first encountered him during the course of an earlier investigation and so Brough took Darren's assertions that he was 'pretty trim' with an entire sackful of salt.

"Right then, what next?"

"Back to work for me," said Brough. "After a shower, back at mine."

"Sounds good. The shower part, I mean, not the work." The light of hope in Darren's eyes did not go unnoticed.

"What?" said Brough.

"Could I…"

"What?"

"Could I come with you? Back to yours. Only my hot water's packed in and—"

"I suppose," said Brough. "Can't have you stinking like a galley slave for Mel, can we? I'll race you. Once around the bandstand and then back up the road."

"You're on!" Darren laughed and sprang away.

"Bloody cheat!" laughed Brough, giving chase.

But when they reached the bandstand, a hexagonal concrete platform with a dark brick perimeter, all thoughts of the race and showers and everything else vanished like a soap bubble pricked by a finger.

There was a dead man lying on the rostrum, his arms and legs stretched and tied to follow a chalk design. A length of plastic-coated clothes line was tight around his neck. His eyes bulged from their sockets, staring blankly at the sky, and his tongue, blue and swollen, poked out of his mouth like a shy tortoise.

"What the fuck?" Darren came to a standstill.

"Stay back." Brough held out an arm as a cordon. He took out his phone and speed-dialled Wheeler, without taking his eyes off the poor bastard staked out in front of him. Brough couldn't help feeling a rush of guilt.

This is what I wished for, he realised. And now this poor bastard's paid the price.

6.

Wheeler summoned the Serious team in from their bullshit other duties at once. They convened in an upstairs room at Dedley nick which, like a childhood home, seemed smaller now they had returned to it. Wheeler's uniform was still dusted with flour, stained with eggs and dripping with milk.

"Is it Pancake Day?" laughed Stevens.

"It is now the tosser's arrived," Wheeler retorted. "Right, let's get you all apprised of what we know so far. David."

She ceded the floor to Brough who got to his feet, which were still in his trainers. He was also still wearing his tracksuit and his sweat-damp hair was ruffled from a quick rub with a towel.

"Victim is a middle-aged male. Caucasian. Initial thoughts are the cause of death is asphyxiation – and no," he looked pointedly at Stevens, "it probably wasn't a strangle-wank."

Stevens looked disappointed.

"What then?" Harry Henry was on the edge of his seat.

"Garrotted. With a washing-line."

"Urgh." Harry Henry shrank back. He ran a finger under his shirt collar.

Brough continued. "We'll know more when we get the lab results."

Pattimore interrupted. "What's his name?"

Brough reddened. After all this time, he still couldn't look his ex in the eye. Pattimore had been attending anger management classes and a course of Cognitive Behavioural Therapy and all the rest of it, but it still hurt. Brough tamped down his personal issues and answered in a clipped, professional tone.

"Ah, yes. The wallet found in his jacket indicates he is Paul Barker, local entrepreneur."

The team pulled faces; they had never heard of him.

"And what about how he was found?" Miller chimed in. "And where he was found?"

"On the bandstand in Field Park, do you mean?"

"Yes."

"The body was arranged to fit a crude outline of a five-pointed star."

"Pentagram." This was Stevens. The others turned their heads in astonishment. "It bloody well is! A pentagram. They use them in devil worship."

"Who do?" said Harry Henry.

"No, mate. Not Voodoo. Devil worship. Satanism."

"And how the fuck do you know this?" Wheeler was surprised. "I know I've told you to go to hell a thousand times but I didn't think you'd actually fucking been."

"Saw it in a film," Stevens shrugged. "*To The Devil A Dildo*. It was ace. Lots of lezzing up."

The others emitted groans; they might have guessed.

"How many more times?" Wheeler threw up her hands – and a cloud of flour in the process, "Pornography is not like real life. If it was I wouldn't have to spend half my Saturday waiting in for a bastard plumber to show up."

"No, no," said Brough. "I think Ben might be onto something here." He scribbled a quick sketch and showed it to Stevens. "Was the star in the film like this?"

"Yeah! From what I remember. Of course, I wasn't focussing on the fucking scenery."

"Ugh," said Miller.

"Right," said Wheeler. "We need to find out what we might be dealing with here. Harry, hit the books. Wiki-fucking-pedia if you have to. Brough, Miller, find out more about Mr Barker – perhaps he was into all sorts. A cult, maybe. Fucking hell," she ran a hand down her face, whitening it like a clown's. "That's all we fucking need in this town. Go on," she jerked a floury thumb toward the exit in time-honoured tradition, "Fuck off."

Brough and Miller, closely followed by Harry Henry, fucked off. Pattimore and Stevens remained.

"What about us, Chief?" Pattimore was eager. "Do you want us to go to the lab, fetch the results?"

"Good idea, Jason. Go on; off you fuck."

***

Logger sloped off; the others had gone back to school. That specky twat Callum wotsit had suggested it would be good to show their faces around the place in order to establish an alibi. Dogger and Bonk had followed blindly and that irked Logger considerably. He regarded himself as the putative leader of the gang and did not like being elbowed aside. Especially by a specky twat.

He skulked off, taking umbrage behind a disused outbuilding that was rumoured to have been a bike shed. Who rides a bike to school these days? Nobody; that's who. The roads are too busy with four-by-fours, dropping off the kids.

Satisfied he was alone, Logger took out his phone. He sent a text message.

Safe to call

Seconds later, the phone buzzed and shook. The rapidity of the response always startled Logger, no matter how he steeled himself for it.

"Hello," he said and found – as always – a sudden need to clear his throat.

"Guess who," said a deep voice in his ear. The words were followed by a laugh, although there was no humour in it.

"Look, I know what you'm going to say—" Logger tried to pre-empt a litany of his failings.

"I doubt that," rumbled the caller. There was a metallic tone to the voice; Logger guessed it was electronically distorted for the sake of anonymity. He had no clue who the caller was, but as long as the money kept coming, that was fine by him. "I doubt that entirely. If you knew what I was about to say, we should have no need of telephones."

"Um, no, I suppose."

"Humour me. What was I about to say?"

"Ah – well – um…"

"I doubt I should be so inarticulate."

"Yes, well…" Logger composed himself. "You were about to tell me what a balls-up we'd made of it."

"I doubt I should be so vulgar but I take your meaning. Continue."

"And that going to the supermarket was a big mistake. And recruiting the new chap was an even bigger mistake."

"I'll stop you there. I've heard enough. You are in error in every respect. On the contrary, dear boy – the visit to the supermarket was a triumph!"

"It was?"

"Undoubtedly! And as for the latest recruit, he has excellent potential. You must cultivate him."

"If that means burying him in my grandad's allotment, you're on."

"Cut the levity. The new boy is crucial for the next phase."

"If you say so."

"Say so I do. Take him under your capable wing. Teach him and, more importantly, learn from him."

Logger sneered. As if the specky twat could teach me anything!

"He's a weirdo," he complained.

"We are all individuals."

"No. He's proper weird. Worse than ever since the initiation."

There was silence. "Initiation," the caller said flatly.

"Yes. The other night. I don't know what you did but it's pushed his buttons all right."

"When was this?"

"The other night. Out on the field."

"My dear boy, I told you that was postponed. If you have taken the initiative and carried out matters for yourself—"

"I never!" said Logger.

"Then you told him what to expect and he imagined it…" the caller was thinking out loud.

"We never breathed a word," Logger defended himself and his gang.

"Hmm," the low voice rumbled like a roll on timpani. "Be that as it may. Look after him. You're going to need him. Now, tell me, step by step, what went down at the supermarket. I think I'm going to enjoy this."

But by the time Logger reached the end of his account, the caller was incensed.

"So, you are telling me no one knows who you are or where you're from?"

"We was very careful."

"Not a glimpse of a school badge or a flash of a school tie?"

"Not a sausage!"

The caller swore. Logger was both amused and terrified.

"Let us hope, for your sake, the attendant police officers are not as thick as you."

The caller disconnected. Logger stared at his phone. He felt an urge to smash it against the wall, to stomp on the pieces. But he didn't. It occurred to him that whatever he did to the device would be visited upon his body.

He strode toward the main building, feeling a sudden need to be among people. The bell rang, heralding home time. Kids boiled from the exits like maggots from a corpse. The image made him shudder.

"Alright, Log?"

Logger yelped. Dogger was at his elbow. "Coming down the park? Apparently there's a dead body there."

Logger felt sick. "Who says?"

"Callum."

"I might have known. How does he know?"

Dogger shrugged. "He's got an app. Latest news."

Yeah, that'd be right. The specky twat wouldn't have games or porn like normal people.

"Might be worth a squint, I suppose."

"Bonk's already gone. I said we'd meet him there."

"OK..." Logger scowled. Another decision taken without his say-so! He thrust his hands into the pockets of his hoody and balled them into fists.

***

The clean-up crew at *CostBusters* worked like ravenous vultures on carrion, picking the aisles bare of debris. It struck Charlie West that they would be the people to call to tidy up after you'd committed bloody murder which, given his current frame of mind was not too remote a possibility. He ducked into the staff toilets, shut himself in a stall and pulled out his phone. His call was diverted directly to voicemail, adding to his frustration.

"Listen to me, you little shit!" he growled. "What the fuck was all that in aid of in my work today? I've told you before and I'll tell you again: you and your no-mark friends are to keep away! Stay in fucking school, for fuck's sake. If I'd caught hold of you, I'd've handed you over to the coppers without batting an eyelid. You do know that, don't you? I can't – I won't have you fucking up this job for me. Go and get your kicks somewhere else – no, scratch that. Stay in bloody school and learn how to behave. Christ!"

His anger spent, Charlie slumped against the back of the door. "Look, I know it hasn't been easy on you, Nathan, since Mom...

And I'm doing my best for you, I really am, but you've got to meet me halfway. So no more arsing around, OK? Listen, I'll be finished at six. I'll bring us something nice back for tea, all right? We can watch a film, all right? See you later."

He disconnected.

Across town, in Field Park, his brother saw he had a message. He deleted it at once, unplayed and unheeded.

7.

Brough and Miller found themselves heading back to the larger, more well-to-do houses sooner than they would have liked. But at least they weren't distributing leaflets this time – not that the gruesome murder of a local businessman was in any way a consolation.

Miller pulled up outside Paul Barker's house, a tasteful detached property with pampas trees stationed in a line between its garden and next door's. Brough nodded at the exotic plants.

"And they try to tell us there's no such thing as climate change."

"Who does?" said Miller.

There was a car on the drive, a Bentley, expensive but not ostentatious. Barker had not been overtly flashy with the wealth he had accumulated from his factory.

A light was on in the front room. The newly-widowed Mrs Barker was at home.

"At least she's been told," said Miller as they reached the front door. "She has been informed, hasn't she?"

"I hope so," said Brough. "A couple of uniforms will have been around earlier."

He rang the doorbell.

"Worst part of the job," said Miller. "Telling somebody their loved one is dead."

"Yes," said Brough.

"Even worse when you have to say they've been horribly murdered, like he was. Tied down. Garrotted. With a bloody washing-line of all things. Horrible." She shuddered.

"Er – Miller…"

50

The front door had opened. A middle-aged woman in leopard print and gold chains was staring with bloodshot eyes at the couple on her doorstep.

"Oops," said Miller.

Brough flashed his i.d. and introduced himself and his colleague.

"You'd better come in," said Mrs Barker with a wet sniff.

"Wipe your feet, Miller," Brough advised in a whisper. "You've already put one of them well and truly in it."

Mrs Barker led the detectives into a reception room dominated by a black leather suite. On a glass coffee table with gilded legs stood a half-empty (or half-full, if that's your inclination) bottle of sherry and a single glass. Mrs Barker gestured to the armchairs, perching her narrow behind on the sofa's central cushion.

"This is about my husband, isn't it? Oh, of course it is! What else would it be about?"

She reached for the glass, her hand visibly shaking.

"We are sorry," said Brough, "at this difficult time but we need to look into your husband's background in order to help us piece together what happened."

Mrs Barker nodded. She cupped the glass of sherry in both hands as though it would warm them. "Tell me," she took a sip to steel herself. "Did he suffer?"

Brough and Miller exchanged glances. Before either of them could form a response, Mrs Barker let out a bitter laugh.

"I hope he did! I hope he bloody suffered! The stingy fucker! I hope it hurt a lot! I hope he was terrified! No – I hope he was humiliated."

She downed the rest of the glass and poured herself another. "I mean, look at this place," she made an expansive gesture. Her overfilled glass sloshed some of its contents on the deep-pile rug.

"It's nice," said Miller.

"Bollocks," said Mrs Barker. "The money he made! We could have been living somewhere nice. Like Solihull. Or Little Aston.

But, oh, no. We stayed in this shithole because he said he was a Dedley man through and through. Like that means anything. Tell me, Inspector, do the words 'tight-fisted arsehole' mean anything to you?"

Miller laughed; Brough remained inscrutable.

"We could have had villas in the south of France, a lodge in Val D'Isere. But, oh, no, he wouldn't let me spend a penny. Do you know what that's like?"

Miller squirmed. "Actually, I could do with a comfort break."

Brough scowled.

"Through there, past the stairs."

Miller hurried out. Mrs Barker's eyes bore into Brough's.

"Did you never meet my husband?"

"I can't say I had the pleasure."

Another bitter laugh. "Because you look the sort. I can spot them. I've acquired the knack. I couldn't when I married him but I bloody well can now."

Brough shifted uncomfortably. "Sort?"

"He had one of them wotsits. An app. For finding like-minded individuals. Thought I didn't know about it, but I did. Tried to tell me his late-night excursions were jogs around the park. But he never seemed to get any fitter."

"An app?" Brough prompted, pencil poised at his notebook.

"What's this?" said Miller, breezing back in. "A nap?"

"App, Miller. Like those interminable bubble games you're always playing."

"Oh," Miller sat back down. "Level eighty-one last night," she said proudly. "What app's this?"

"My husband had one," said the widow, her words beginning to slur. "For picking up benders."

"Oh," said Miller. "Like MINCR, do you mean?"

"That's the one!" Mrs Barker raised her glass in congratulation. "You should be a detective, love."

Miller beamed; Brough scowled again.

"And your husband left the house last night on one of his excursions?"

"Must have done. I was a-bed. We have separate rooms, you see. Like that wasn't a tell-tale sign! And I believed him when he said it was on account of my snoring."

She recharged her glass. "So, d'you think it was one of them, one of his *jogging friends* who did him in. It'd serve him right."

"We're not in a position to discuss that," said Brough. He got to his feet so Miller did the same. "Mrs Barker, do you mind if we have a look around? Your husband's things – did he have a home office here?"

"Knock yourselves out," Mrs Barker sat back and slumped like a discarded marionette. "He's got a den upstairs. In what should have been the kiddies' room. If we'd had any." She waved her glass in the general direction of the ceiling and then licked the resulting spillage from her thumb.

"Thank you," said Brough. Miller followed him out.

"Well, I wasn't expecting that," he muttered as they climbed the stairs.

"What? Her reaction? You don't think she's a suspect, do you? She might be! She seems pretty fed up. All his money's hers now, I should think. There's a motive for you."

Miller grinned, pleased with herself.

"No," said Brough, trying a door. It opened onto a room decorated in garish pink. A theatrical dressing-room mirror dominated one wall. Over the four-poster bed, a framed poster of *Hello, Dolly!* "Don't you read the papers, Miller? Barker's firm's in a bit of a hole. You could say the bottom's falling out of the market."

Miller frowned; she didn't get it.

"He manufactured toilets, Miller."

"Oh. So, business has gone down the pan!"

Brough ignored the quip. "What do you think? His room or hers?"

"His, deffo," Miller took it all in. "So, what was it?"

"What was what?"

"What was it what you weren't expecting?"

"Oh! Just took me by surprise, Miller."

"What did?"

"You did. Knowing about MINCR."

Miller beamed. "It's not all about birds throwing themselves at pigs, you know."

"No," said Brough. "That's TINDER."

***

Brough called Wheeler and told her it might be worth looking in Barker's mobile – it was among the personal effects found on the businessman's body – to see if any of his contacts, particularly those in his pick-up apps might lead somewhere.

"Felch me and belch me," Wheeler groaned. "Is every fucker gay these days?"

"What a wonderful world that would be," said Brough.

Wheeler snorted. "I'll get Harry to do it. Spice up his life a bit. He must be bored shitless sorting through those files."

She rang off and went in search of Harry Henry.

"Nothing here..." said Miller, replacing a pair of fluffy pink handcuffs in the bedside drawer. "Although he has got quite a collection of double-ended dildos."

"Stop salivating, Miller."

"And, oh!" Miller's hands seized on a flyer. "He was a DICWAD. Remember them?"

"Of course I remember them!" Brough snapped. "How could I forget?" A previous case had involved the Dedley Independent Chorus With Amateur Dramatics Society. and Brough dreaded to think what production they were murdering next.

"They'm doing *Murder in the Cathedral*, apparently," Miller read the blurb.

Brough had to admit that was classier than their usual output.

"Reimagined in a hip-hop setting," Miller continued.

"Fuck the DICWADS, Miller," Brough sneered, "And come and have a look at this."

She joined Brough at the window. It overlooked the back garden, a neatly trimmed lawn bisected by a path that was lined with cod classical statuary.

"What am I looking at? It's nice. Classy. They must get a man in."

"Not that. Next door."

Miller strained to see. "Oh. That one's not so nice. Bit overgrown. Cluttered, I'd say."

"And the other side."

Miller pressed her cheek against the pane. "That one's OK, I suppose."

"It's not your appraisal of the gardens I want, Miller – insightful though it is."

"What then?"

"One of the three gardens before us is different."

"They'm all different."

"Well, yes, but one of them lacks something the other two have."

"A water feature!"

"No, Miller. Look!"

"It's getting dark," Miller waxed defensive. "Stop pissing about with guessing games and tell me."

Brough chuckled. "You sound like Wheeler when you're narked."

"Stop fucking narking me then. What am I not seeing?"

"A washing-line!" said Brough. "The Barkers have one. The neighbours on this side have one. But the neighbours on the other..."

"So? It doesn't mean – Lots of people don't have washing-lines. Spin dryer and a clothes horse by the radiator does for me."

"Well, yes, but remember the murder weapon, Miller…"

Miller's eyebrows dipped. "He was garrotted."

"With…"

Miller's jaw dropped.

"You see!"

"Oh, it could just be a coincidence."

"Possibly, but we'd be fools not to look into it."

"I suppose."

"No suppose about it. Come on; let's leave the merry widow to her sherry and give next door a knock."

They headed down to the hall.

"How are we going to do it?" Miller asked, with the light of possibility in her eyes. "Pose as representatives from a leading brand of washing powder and say we'm conducting a survey about people's laundry habits?"

"Actually, Miller, I was thinking we could just turn up as police."

***

The sun was also going down on the car park at Priory High School. Only two cars were present: Stevens's Ford Capri and a well-preserved Morris Minor. The vintage car was the pride and joy of Deputy Headteacher Alfred Abbott; the detectives were interviewing him in his office. The CCTV footage from the supermarket was playing on the screen of Mr Abbott's desktop.

"One more time, please," said D C Pattimore, commandeering the mouse so he could replay the recording. "Sorry to keep you behind after school."

"Ha!" said Stevens. "It's like fucking karma or something."

Both Pattimore and Abbott ignored him and kept their attention on the screen.

"It's quite all right," said Alfred Abbott. "Invariably, I'm the last to leave. Long after the cleaning staff have worked their wonders, most nights."

Pattimore looked sideways at the balding, slightly built man and couldn't tell if his smile was tinged with pride or sadness. "And you're quite sure you don't recognise any of the youths involved?"

Abbott pursed his thin lips. "Need I point out they are all wearing hooded jackets?"

"No, you needn't," said Pattimore.

"Wait! There! Freeze it!" Abbott pointed a finger at a fuzzy figure. "Go back – just a tad."

Pattimore manoeuvred the mouse. The action on screen lurched into rewind. Stevens laughed to see spilled milk gather itself into a carton and fly through the air and into a hand.

"Stop it there!" Mr Abbott's finger tapped the screen. "That belligerent stance! I would know it anywhere. I have had cause to make that fellow stand up in Assembly many times and I recognise the slope of those narrow shoulders."

"You know him!" Stevens marvelled. "Even without seeing his mug?"

"Inspector Stevens," Mr Abbott gave the detective a patronising smile. "It is in my interests to know every single one of the children who walk through our gates. I have been employed at this school all my adult life. Further to that, I was a pupil here myself. There is nothing that goes on here about which I do not know."

Stevens found himself wilting beneath the deputy head's scrutiny even though the detective was almost two feet taller than the didact.

"So…" Pattimore's pencil was poised. "What's his name?"

"Lawrence. Logan Lawrence, known colloquially, I believe, as Logger."

Pattimore jotted all this down. "And do you have an address for this Logan Lawrence?"

"Not memorised, of course, but it is the work of seconds to access the database."

"Good. We should very much like to have a chinwag with Logan Lawrence."

"I doubt you will get much from him," Abbott heaved his shoulders. "A few Neanderthal grunts is the best you can hope for. I am not saying the boy is what we used to call *remedial* but, well, sometimes I despair of the youth of today and most of the time I despair for the school. I mean, how are we supposed to maintain our ranking in the league tables when our clientele is of that – that—" he waved at the frozen image, "calibre."

"You sound very passionate," Pattimore observed.

"I am! This school has been my life and I cannot bear to see it failing."

"Is it failing?"

"Well, no. Not quite. Not yet. But it will, the way things are going."

"And which way are things going?"

Mr Abbott exhaled a lengthy sigh. "I'm afraid, gentlemen, that information is not yet within the public domain."

Pattimore glanced around at their surroundings. "We're in a private office."

"Let me just say change is coming."

"Not all change is bad."

The deputy head shook his deputised head. Weariness clouded his features. "I have seen all sorts of things come and go. First, we merged with the girls' high school – it's a car park now on the other side of the field – then we lost our status as a grammar school, but we mustered our mettle and worked hard to become the best damned comprehensive in the whole of Dedley. We retained as much of our former grammar school prestige as we could. Then we were amalgamated with Squirrel's Hole High, lost the old girls' high building and it has all been downhill from there, I am afraid.

Oh, we got a couple of new wings built on and the Science block, in order to accommodate the additional intake – you may have noticed the garish red brick add-ons. Quite at odds with some of the older parts of the structure – old Emmanuel would spin in his grave. He was the first headmaster. The school was established over four hundred years ago to lift the boys of Dedley out of ignorance and want."

He tried not to notice D I Stevens picking his nose.

"You see, in the old days – I mean, the more recent old days, not the first days of Baxter Emmanuel – the likes of Logan Lawrence would have gone to Squirrel's Hole where he could have run amok and no harm done to their examination results. He and his cronies might even have come away with a C.S.E. in Woodwork rather than infecting some of our brighter students with their indolence, impudence and insolence. I have always been of the opinion that the Squirrel's Hole refugees should have been sent down to Hangham – which is in a permanent state of 'special measures' – but they are full up too. Oversubscribed! That dump!"

Stevens yawned; Pattimore nudged him.

"You mentioned his cronies," Pattimore prompted, demonstrating his talent for sifting out the pertinent information from the deputy head's waffle. "Are you able to identify any of them?"

"Not from the playback, no. But our friend Logger is invariably in the company of Duncan Dogberry, a.k.a. Dogger, and a third boy who displays all the perspicacity of a mouldering potato. His real name eludes me, I am afraid, but he goes by the informal moniker of Bonk."

Stevens sniggered. "Logger, Dogger and Bonk! Weren't they the three pixies on the cereal box?"

"I would say imps rather than pixies," sniffed Mr Abbott. "Fledgling demons."

Pattimore scribbled a few hasty notes. "Now, this change that's coming."

Mr Abbott shook his head. "Doomed to failure, right from the off. My school has become a shithouse, a repository for all the turds pushed out by the uncaring parents of the borough. Dressing it up in glitter is not going to change that."

"Mr Abbott, what are you talking about?"

"It's that supermarket, isn't it?" he spat at the screen. "Or rather its brash and boorish owner. He wants to sponsor my school when it turns into an – an – I can barely bring myself to say the word – an *academy*!"

He pulled a face that suggested he had just French-kissed a lemon.

Stevens blinked. "And what's wrong with that?"

Mr Abbott's face darkened. "That oaf – and more than a few oafs in our benighted government – seem to think one can run a school as a business. It goes against every educational tenet and belief I hold dear. It—"

Pattimore stood, cutting him off. "Well, we won't go into all of that right now. Thank you for your time, Mr Abbott. You have been very helpful."

Mr Abbott inclined his head in a bow. "Always happy to assist the boys in blue. Even," he cocked an eyebrow at Stevens's tan leather jacket, "when they are not actually in blue. Allow me to walk you out."

At the door, Stevens turned back to prolong the meeting. "Almost forgot!" he rolled his eyes at his own absent-mindedness. "Does the name Barker mean anything to you? Paul Barker?"

Mr Abbott's face was inscrutable. "He is one of our governors. The chair, no less."

"Not no more he ain't," said Stevens flatly. "He's dead."

"Oh?" Mr Abbott's expression did not change. "I am sorry to hear it."

"Murdered," Stevens continued. "They found him this morning. Strangled in the park."

"Oh, dear."

"Garrotted, actually."

"That is unpleasant."

"Not half."

"This is distressing news," said Mr Abbott, although neither detective thought he looked particularly distressed.

"Goodnight, sir," said Pattimore with a curt smile.

"Yeah," added Stevens.

They did not speak until they were ensconced in Stevens's Capri.

"Boring old fart," was Stevens's assessment. "Imagine spending all your life in one job."

Pattimore flicked through his notes. "We need to find this Logger kid."

"Didn't seem to like kids much, did he? Why does he stick with the job if he don't like kids? Miserable git. It ain't the kids' fault they come from depraved backgrounds."

"Deprived," Pattimore muttered.

"Fuck off, *Brough*! Did you see his face? When we told him Barker was dead. He didn't seem all that surprised. And I'm sure I saw a little bit of a smile creeping onto his lips…"

"We must be careful not to read too much into that," Pattimore advised. "People react in all sorts of ways to bad news."

"Seems to me he was trying very hard not to take it as good news."

"And why would he do that? What could he have to gain by the death of a school governor?"

"The chair, no less," Stevens mocked Abbott's pompous tones. "Something to think about it, ain't it? At the pub."

"All right," said Pattimore. "The pub."

***

By the time those pixies, those fledgling demons, Logger, Dogger and Bonk got to Field Park, it was all cordoned off and crawling with coppers. The bandstand was surrounded by a huge, blue tent and SOCOs in white bodysuits busied themselves in and out of it.

"What a swizz," Logger muttered.

"He's probably miles away by now," added Dogger. "Being cut up on a slab."

"Ugh," said Bonk.

Dogger brightened. "If we hurry up, we might be home in time for the local news. Bound to be something on there."

"Like on the telly?" Bonk frowned. "Is Dedley going to be on the telly?"

"Bound to be," said Dogger.

"Wow!" Bonk enthused. Their home town hadn't attracted much media attention since that time when they were making a film about a hospital or something and that Oscar Buzz had come over from Hollywood and everything. "I'd best be off any road," Bonk's face clouded. "My brother's going to kill me."

"Then Dedley'll be on tomorrow night and all," said Logger.

"Coo," said Bonk.

He and Dogger hurried away from the park gates. Logger dawdled. He was reluctant to go home, certain the Boss would call him. Yes, well, the Boss could call him anywhere, at any time, but at home, Logger felt confined. Hemmed in. Things were spiralling out of control. Cause disruption, he'd been told. It was what he was being paid for. But now there was a murder. The very man they were supposed to target next had turned up dead in Field Park. Logger paled; it had been a narrow escape. If they'd gone through with the plan, if they'd sent those photographs...

That would have been the specky twat's job. Uploading the photos to Barker's laptop, his smartphone and his 'cloud', whatever that was.

Now there was no need. The good ship *Blackmail* had been scuppered and sunk before they had boarded it.

Thank fuck.

Perhaps with the bloke dead and blackmail no longer an option, they wouldn't need the specky twat in the gang anymore. It wasn't as though he was a proper member anyway. Where was he now, for example? He hadn't wanted to come and get a look at the body, the chicken shit. He'd mumbled something and buggered off. Urgent Maths homework or some bollocks. The specky twat.

The phone in Logger's pocket vibrated, making him jump. Guess who! He considered declining the call or letting it ring through to voicemail, but that would only defer the unpleasantness.

"Yo!" he answered, his voice cracking.

"Good evening, Lawrence. I learn from the news that the next phase of our plan has been derailed."

"I don't think it was a train crash."

"Please abandon all attempts at humour. With Barker gone, we can move to the next stage. You still have the photographs?"

"Um, yeah. They'm on the new kid's phone."

"Excellent. Then we simply swap recipients. How familiar are you with Dedley Council?"

The question threw Logger. He forced himself to concentrate. "I know me mom pays them rent and moans when they don't take the rubbish."

"In that case, I am sending you a file. A photo of the man and his contact details. Get those snaps uploaded by tomorrow night. We must keep applying pressure."

"Yeah, but—"

"No buts, Lawrence. You will, of course, receive your next emolument when the thing is done."

"Emo what now?"

"Payment – Perhaps if you attended a few more lessons, you'd know that."

The line went dead. Logger poked his tongue out at the screen. If I went to school all day, Mr Boss Man, I wouldn't be able to do half the stuff you pay me to do.

The phone buzzed – a raspberry in response to Logger's own. An email had come through. Logger decided he would rather wait until he was safely shut up in his room before he opened it.

***

"Pasta's ready!" Melanie Miller called out. Steam clouded the kitchen sink while she shook the spaghetti in a colander. "Darren!" she called again.

There was no response. He did not emerge from the bedroom until Miller had plated up the food and poured drinks. Wine for herself and water for him.

"Sorry, Mel; I was on the phone." He waved his mobile as evidence.

"It's all right," said Miller, sharply sucking a strand of spaghetti.

Darren sat and tucked a napkin into the collar of his polo shirt. "Looks lovely. Thanks." He pushed the food around, twisting it onto his fork. "Is this…"

"It's not real mince," Miller assured him. "It's that soya protein stuff. David recommends it."

"Ah!" He tucked into the meal with more gusto. Miller wondered whether it was because of the healthy nature of the food or because of who had endorsed it.

She was willing to bet that was who he had been calling. Detective Inspector David bleeding Brough. Handsome, homosexual David bleeding Brough.

She took a gulp of wine, steeling herself to broach the subject head on. "So, how did it go with David?"

"Who?"

"David Brough. You had a training session with him today."

"Oh, him!" Darren chuckled. "All right. Good, actually. Right up until we found that dead body."

"Oh. Yes. And will you be seeing him again?"

"Shouldn't think so. Wasn't planning on going to the funeral."

"Not the dead body! Brough! David!"

"Um, I expect so. We haven't fixed anything up for deffo yet. I expect you'll be busy."

"Will I?"

"Both of you. Because of the dead body."

"Oh. Oh, yes. Crusty bread?" she proffered the basket.

"No, ta, love; you know how it bloats me right up."

They finished the spag bol in silence – apart from Darren's grunts of appreciation. Miller eyed her boyfriend through the prism of her wine glass. She supposed she should be relieved he wasn't having protracted phone calls with Brough, who blatantly fancied Darren, and for whom she had once held a candle…

She drained her glass, drowning those thoughts.

But if not Brough, then who the bloody hell had Darren been speaking to for so long?

***

Before bed, Brough, wrapped in his voluminous bathrobe, attempted to make a Skype call to Oscar. He couldn't work out if it would be lunch- or teatime where Oscar was filming – *What am I thinking*, he laughed? *Oscar's American; they don't do teatime.*

There was no answer. Oscar was invariably busy and when they did get to connect it was because he was the one to make the call. There was no chance of that million-dollar smile tonight then. Looking at a DVD cover was not the same.

Probably for the best, Brough reflected as he crawled under the duvet. *Let him see me when I've shed a few pounds – several tons, in fact! I am such a fucking narwhal.*

Brough forced himself to think of the unfolding murder case in order to distract himself from what he perceived to be his gigantic circumference.

Oscar's not the only one to go global—

No, stop it!

Think of the dead man on the bandstand. Who would do that to him? Was he a random victim, fallen prey to a cult? Or was he the specific target of ritualised slaughter?

Oddly, these thoughts did nothing to help Brough get to sleep.

***

Mrs Phillips intercepted her son on the landing. "Callum? What are you doing up? It's the middle of the night."

Callum grunted: the language of the teenager. Then he translated for his mother's benefit. "Getting a drink of water. Not a crime, is it?"

Mrs Phillips frowned. She didn't care for his tone lately. It was his age, she supposed. And the company he was keeping at that school.

"You're still dressed, love."

"You want me to strip off? Perv!"

"No, I'm just saying you should be in bed. Asleep."

"I was working," Callum snapped. His mother could be such an idiot sometimes. How she managed to reach her great age (forty-six) he couldn't imagine.

"You can work too hard, you know." She reached for the sleeve of his hoody but withdrew her hand as though repelled by a force field.

"Make your mind up," he shrugged her off all the same. "Can't win, can I? I'm not studying enough. I'm studying too much."

"That's not – I'm just – worried. The police were around earlier. Two detectives." She looked for a reaction but there was no discernible change in Callum's slouched posture, his long-suffering scowl.

"What the hell did they want?"

"It's bad news—"

"Not Dad?"

Mr Phillips was often away on business. That was part of the problem, thought Mrs Phillips. I can't handle everything on my own.

"No! Not your father. It's Mr Barker, next door. He's dead, love."

"Oh. Him."

"You don't seem surprised."

"It was on the news. He was a prick anyway."

"Callum! I didn't bring you up to use such language. And about the dead!"

"Well, he was." Callum glowered at his mother. "I'm fetching my water now."

Mrs Phillips gave up. "Goodnight, love," she said sadly and withdrew into her bedroom. Callum didn't even mutter a reply. He hurried down the stairs to the kitchen.

He unlocked the back door and slipped out into the night.

Mrs Phillips lay awake, listening, waiting for her increasingly wayward son to come back upstairs and return to his room. After a while, she wondered if she had dozed off and missed him. After about an hour, she could bear it no longer. She sprang from her bed.

Callum's door was open and his bed was empty.

"Callum?"

She tripped down the stairs. The kitchen light was on. The sink was empty. No glass of water had been filled that night.

The back door was unbolted.

"Callum…"

Mrs Phillips peered out into the back garden as if expecting to find him there.

8.

Wheeler held the team briefing early the next morning. The murder victim was something of a bigshot in certain circles, not least of which was Dedley Chamber of Commerce. As ever, money means connections and connections mean power. Several councillors had already bent Superintendent Ball's ear, applying pressure to get the killer or killers brought to justice.

Maybe if they weren't spending all the fucking council tax on twenty recycling bins of many colours for every fucking house in the borough, the police might be better resourced. Honestly! You only need one bin for recycling; let the fuckers sort through it at the rubbish tip, for fuck's sake.

"Um, Chief?" It was Harry Henry who brought Wheeler's attention back into the room. "You were saying?"

"Was I? Oh, yes." Wheeler extended her arm in what, to a casual observer, might be misconstrued as a fascist salute, in order to point the remote control at the video projector suspended from the ceiling. A shot of the bandstand in Field Park appeared, the victim's face superimposed on Wheeler's own while behind her a Wheeler-shaped black hole menaced the dead man. "Fuck it," she muttered and sidestepped out of the way.

"Speak to me, people. What am we looking at here? What am we not seeing?"

"Victim is male," offered Miller.

"Mid-to-late forties," added Pattimore. "Fifty at a push."

"Name: Paul Barker, founder of *Barker's Bogs*, establishing his factory in 1993," Brough reeled off the facts from his notebook.

"Jesus wiped," Wheeler groaned. "I told you all that shit yesterday. Nobody got nothing new to bring to the party or shall we all phone our mummies and daddies and ask them to pick us up early?"

"He was garrotted," said Stevens, "with a standard length clothes line, available from several outlets in the town. Just about every-fucking-where, in fact."

"Owner untraceable then?"

"You'd think so," Stevens continued with a smirk. "I've asked the lab to check for prints."

Wheeler shook her head. "Our man could've been wearing gloves. If he had any fucking sense."

"Yes…" Stevens's moustache twitched as his smirk grew larger. "But whoever used it to peg out the washing probably wouldn't have. We might be able to trace the owner."

Everyone stared at him. Stevens wilted a little under the collective gaze of the team.

"Well, spit on my clit and tell me it's Tuesday!" Wheeler marvelled. "You might actually be on to something there, Benny-boy. Will wonders never fucking cease?"

Brough and Miller exchanged glances, both thinking the same thought.

"Actually, Chief," said Brough, "we think we might know where to start looking. It might be coincidental but Barker's next-door neighbours have no washing-line."

Wheeler's eyes widened like twin balloons inflating. "This is too good to be fucking true!" She clapped her hands and rubbed them together. Visions of closing the case on the first day of the investigation danced in her head. That would show those shitheads, those penny-pinching, pen-pushers what a crack team she had!

"Excellent! We might catch the bastard by teatime. Yes, Harry?" She turned her grin to the detective whose finger was raised like a nervous child asking leave to go to the toilet.

"Um," Harry used that finger to push his spectacles back up the bridge of his nose. "I've been looking into that five-pointed star stuff."

"Eh? Oh, never mind that shit," Wheeler waved a dismissive hand. "We can ask the bastard all about that when we've collared him."

Harry Henry slumped in his seat, nursing a folder bulging with research on his lap.

"This could be a record! Murder solved within twenty-four hours. We could be a one-stop cop shop!"

But Wheeler's high spirits were to be short-lived. Superintendent Ball came in.

"I'm afraid," he addressed the group directly, "things may not appear as cut-and-dried as all that."

"Here we fucking go," Wheeler sighed. "Just when you get your chips, some bugger comes along to piss on them."

"What is it, sir?" asked Pattimore.

"You'll forgive me if I don't deliver the news in a Scottish accent as they are wont to do on the old television programmes my wife insists on watching ad nauseam but there has been another murder."

***

Brough and Miller were despatched to the scene: the car park adjacent to the playing field of Priory High School. It was already crawling with forensic detectives, like ants at a picnic. Brough lifted the blue and white plastic tape across the entrance (formerly the gates to Dedley Girls High) so that Miller could duck underneath. He followed her to the eye of the activity, a burned-out Volkswagen Golf.

Brough flashed his i.d. and a forensic photographer pointed him in director of the SOCO in charge.

"Morning," the SOCO nodded to the detectives. "I thought Serious had disbanded."

"Not disbanded," said Brough. "Just moved house. What are we looking at?"

The SOCO sucked air in through his teeth. "Nasty one, this. Worse than that poor sod on the bandstand."

"Who is it?" said Miller. "Do we know?"

"Running the licence plate now but that will only tell us who the car belongs to. There will have to be dental checks before we know the identity of the poor bastard inside. But it's probably the owner. This car park is used mainly by people who work in the town – council offices are just around the corner – and you drive your own car to work, don't you?"

"So, he might work for the council, do you think?" said Brough.

"Or she," said Miller.

"You're right," the SOCO smiled at her. "To question the victim's gender. So badly burned we don't have a clue. Not yet. We'll know more when we get him – or her – out."

"And when will that be?"

The SOCO bristled, detecting a note of impatience in Brough's tone.

"Inspector, you don't appreciate the delicacies of our work. Not only must every aspect of the scene be documented before we can touch anything but the poor bastard is quite literally welded to the interior of the vehicle. The seat, the steering wheel, the dash… It's hard to tell where one begins and the other ends."

"Coo," said Miller. "It must have got quite hot in there."

"Of course it did, Miller. It was a bloody fire! Any idea how it might have started? Are we sure we're dealing with a murder here?"

"Pretty sure," said the SOCO, growing annoyed with the male detective. "And we believe it's linked to the previous one in the park."

"How so?"

"Come and have a squint. Mind where you're treading."

They picked their way closer to the car. A couple of the team was in the process of removing the driver's door. Miller gasped when she glimpsed the unfortunate person inside. A blackened skeleton, crisp and flaking, the mouth gaping in a silent, unending scream. Miller looked away, focussing her attention on the SOCO.

"Burned into the roof is a five-pointed star, such as was found on the bandstand."

Brough and Miller exchanged sidelong glances.

"And how – how was it done?" Miller almost choked; she couldn't bear to look at the car and was trying not to breathe in. She didn't want her brain to identify the scorched and smoky smells she was trying to keep out of her nostrils.

"Best guess is the victim was drenched in petrol – or some other combustible – and set on fire. Perhaps via the sunroof. Would have gone up in an instant – Woof! – and the car would have worked like an oven or kiln."

"Ugh," Miller shuddered.

A woman approached. She beckoned the SOCO aside and showed him something on her tablet.

"Well, well," the SOCO returned to the detectives. "The car is registered to none other than the deputy leader of Dedley Council himself. I am ninety-nine per cent certain our overcooked friend will turn out to be Mr Barry Norwood."

***

Mrs Phillips allowed her tea to steep for longer than usual. She would have preferred a stronger drink but it was too early for booze. Hands shaking, she upended the teapot over her mug and then fumbled the teaspoon, shedding granulated sugar across the worktop. She burst into tears – I haven't even spilled the milk yet.

She sank onto a chair and tried to steady her nerves. The ride to school that morning had been fraught with tension. Callum had been belligerent. Obnoxious, even. She had confiscated his phone – he had left it charging up in the kitchen while he was in the shower and she'd seen her chance. Denying him phone privileges might be the only effective method of disciplining him but so far all it had got her was a lot of invective accompanied by the slamming of doors.

"Give me my fucking phone back, you fucking bitch!" he had spat at her when she pulled up at the school gates.

"Get out," she'd said.

"I fucking hate you," was his parting shot, along with a slam of the passenger door.

Now, in her kitchen, Mrs Phillips was wracked with sobs. What had happened to her sweet little boy? Why was he being so cruel, so horrible?

His phone was on the table in front of her. She couldn't bring herself to touch it. It lay there, dormant, a malevolent slab.

Oh, it serves me right for looking at it, she scolded herself. Serves me right for looking at his private things.

But I was only trying to be a good mum, to find out what's going on. He used to tell me everything – including the passcode to unlock his phone: the year of his birth – and Mrs Phillips was unlikely to forget that.

And there, in the phone's photo gallery, she had seen things that disturbed her. Oh, she'd steeled herself for pornography – he was a teenage boy, after all – but not for the images she had found, pictures taken in real life not downloaded from some grubby website.

There was nothing else for it. She would have to phone his father. So what if he was in a meeting? This was important. This was their son. Their Callum. Their everything.

She reached for the handset for the landline. It took three attempts for her fumbling fingers to tap in the number correctly.

"Bloody hell, Sheila – how many times do I have to—"

"It's Callum!" Sheila Phillips interrupted her husband's tirade. "We have to talk about Callum."

She heard her husband make apologies to whomever he was with. She could almost hear his eyes rolling. He moved to a quieter spot – out in the corridor, she imagined.

"What the hell is this about?" he snapped but there was panic in his voice. "Is he hurt?"

"No! No!" she said quickly. "He called me a fucking bitch today."

"Who did? Our Callum did?"

"Yes! He was horrible."

"That doesn't sound like our Callum."

"That's why I'm phoning. Oh, Donny; it's been awful. The mood swings. The disrespect. And now I've seen things on his phones."

"What things?"

"Photos."

"What photos?"

"Oh, Donny; I'm so worried."

"Sheila!" Don Phillips barked. "Just tell me. What fucking photos?"

"If you're going to start swearing at me as well—"

"Sheila, please. I've got very important clients waiting."

"Arses!" Sheila Phillips cried.

"Some of them, yes, but I have to keep them sweet."

"On his phone! Arses! Three of them."

"Oh, well, he's a teenage lad. Bound to be taking an interest in the female form."

"These are boys' arses! Pale, skinny, flabby, spotty, all sorts. But they're definitely boys' arses. Oh, Donny; where did we go wrong?"

"Fuck's sake, Sheila. You'm making the Grand Canyon out of a couple of bumholes. I'm sure you're worrying about nothing. Listen; I'll phone you later. Just don't embarrass the boy. I'll have a man-to-man talk with him when I get back. Day after tomorrow. Sit tight until then, all right?"

He rang off and returned to his meeting.

Mrs Phillips hurled the handset at the wall.

***

Dennis Lord swivelled in his chair and squeezed a button on his earpiece. His office of chrome and smoked glass overlooked the development of apartment blocks and trendy restaurants around the Birmingham canal basin. You could get bespoke beefburgers now and it would only cost you an arm and a leg. Dennis could remember not many years ago when it had all been derelict factories and warehouses as far as the eye could see, when the canals were stagnant and putrid – a place where supermarket trolleys went to a watery grave. But look at it now! It was amazing how a little investment and entrepreneurship could work miracles and transform a blighted area into a lucrative one. And talk about job creation! People were raking it in, in somewhere in the region of the minimum wage (give or take a couple of quid). Yes, they were all service jobs with little to no hope of advancement but the students and immigrants and immigrant students seemed to quite like a zero-hours contract. At least the ones he employed in the *CostBusters Locale* did. Locale – he had insisted on the 'e' at the end. It made it French. And classy. And meant he could charge between five and ten per cent more for the goods than at his larger stores without a crimp in his conscience. They'm paying for the convenience of a local (*locale*) shop, ain't they?

"Are you there?"

The voice in his ear brought him out of his reverie of self-justification.

"Yes, my love. I'm all yours – if you play your cards right and don't make me sleep on the wet patch."

At the other end of the line, Beatrice Mooney shuddered, almost retching. "Have you seen the news?"

"Only news I need to see, chicken, is how my shares are doing."

"It's Paul. Paul Barker."

"Who?"

"Paul! *Barker's Bogs*. He's been murdered."

"Oh! That would explain why he didn't come to the meeting. Don't you worry your pretty little head about nothing, sweet cheeks. I'll cover what he was planning to put in. The project will still go ahead."

"Um – right." It hadn't been at the forefront of Beatrice Mooney's mind. "That's good of you, Dennis."

"And I'll send the widow a bunch of flowers – No, fuck that. A hamper of the finest produce from our *internationale* range. He did have a Mrs, didn't he?"

Beatrice winced. He'd pronounced it 'internationarly'. "Um, yes. I expect so."

"Because he always struck me as a bit…"

"What?"

"You know. You wouldn't trust him to be a lollipop man. He had that kind of look about him. You know what I mean."

"I'm not sure I do."

"Well, it's full steam ahead. Not going to let one little hiccup get in our way."

"Hiccup? A man is dead!"

"And there's fuck all I can do about it."

Beatrice Mooney sighed. "No, I suppose not. Have you heard from Barry?"

"Who?"

"Barry. Barry Norwood."

"Oh! Barry! Not since the meeting, no. Why? Should I?"

"I've been trying to phone him."

"Oh, have you now?"

"Yes."

"And what for, might I ask?" Dennis snapped. He didn't like it when people had conversations that did not include him. Even though she was miles away, Beatrice Mooney flinched.

"Well, it's – I'm – Listen, Dennis, I'm not sure this is the direction I want to take the school in, and all this business with Paul…"

Dennis Lord roared. "Now, you listen here, you stuck-up bitch. I've already invested a shitload of money in your shithole of a school and, what's worth more, a shitload of my valuable time. Your shithole of a school will become an academy whether you like it or not. Whether you'm working there or not. Am I making myself clear?"

"Y – yes, Dennis."

"Good. This business with Barker – how is it related to our business? It's not. That's how. It's unfortunate but it's nothing to do with us. Tell you what, I'll send you one of them hampers and all. Cheer you up a bit."

Beatrice Mooney hung up.

"Moody cow," said Dennis. He buzzed through to his P.A. "Bridget, love. Send a hamper *internationarly* to that Mooney woman up at the school."

"I'll see to it right away," said Bridget's disembodied voice.

"Oh – and – almost forgot – add a couple of thousand extra reward points to Mrs Barker's loyalty card, would you? Least we can do."

"Yes, sir. Terrible thing—"

"I don't want to be disturbed. I'm working on my big thing."

"Yes, s—"

But Dennis cut her off. He pulled out a set of plans and admired them. A school was one thing but this baby…

In her office in Priory High, Beatrice Mooney chewed at a perfectly manicured fingernail. She refreshed the local news website on her browser. A new headline appeared.

LOCAL MAN BURNT TO A CRISP IN
DEDLEY CAR PARK INFERNO

The accompanying photograph showed the remains of the car and the forensic team swarming around it. And there, beyond the dividing hedge, looming in the distance was Priory High School itself.

Not exactly one for the brochure.

She scrolled through the article. Details were sketchy. The 'local man' was not being named but Beatrice Mooney's stomach was performing cartwheels. A feeling of dread brought her out in a sweat.

She tried Barry Norwood's number again, only to be told by a pre-recorded robot that it was unavailable.

***

In his room, Logger received a call. No prizes for guessing who was calling.

"What the fuck is going on?" the distorted voice barked. Logger had to hold the handset away from his ear.

"How'd you mean?"

"How do I mean? Are you completely ignorant of current events?"

"Oh! That!"

"Yes! That. A second man dead. The second of our targets. Dead."

"It's not my fault—"

"How are you going to coerce, manipulate and blackmail dead men, Lawrence? You're not. That's how."

"But – but – doesn't it – isn't it in your favour?" Logger dared to point out. "Two of the four out of the picture. They can't go through with it now, can they?"

The caller let out a long, weary exhalation.

"No, you little shit, it isn't in my favour. Think about it for a nanosecond, will you? With half the team gone, the whole project could be cancelled."

"But I thought—"

"That's just it: you didn't think. Oh, just lie low for a few days. Let the dust settle. Do nothing until you hear from me. Understood?"

"Y—"

But the line was dead.

"Do nothing" Logger mocked his phone. Oh, I can do that all right. I can do nothing. Twice, if you like.

***

Callum was seething. He slammed the front door and stomped along the path and away from the house, letting his anger lead him. How dare she? How fucking dare she?

He had never seen those photos on his phone before and certainly hadn't taken them. What the hell did she think he was?

It must have been the others. They must have taken pictures of their own arses when they had his phone the other night. Some kind of joke. Part of the initiation, no doubt. Serves me right for not checking, for trusting them.

Logger, Dogger and Bonk, he could forgive. But Mum – never! All those insinuations she made. As if there was anything wrong with being gay – which I'm not, but it wouldn't matter if I was – Where did she go wrong, she kept wailing?

Callum's angry strides took him down the hill toward the town centre, where only rats and litter skittered in the empty marketplace. He carried on, past the council buildings, until he came to the car park, which was still cordoned off. All those poor office workers! Where would they park their cars in the morning?

The school was a dark shadow against the sky. Callum kept walking, keeping the fence to his left. At the bottom of School Road there was a roundabout. Ahead was the Dorothy Beaumont nursing home – Callum's gran had died in there – and beyond, the council estate where his new friends lived. But Callum was not interested in visiting the other members of the gang. Instead, he turned right and onto the park, where the ruins of a 10th century priory – the one that gave the school its name – stood like an abandoned Lego project.

He picked his way past the chicken-wire fencing that guarded the most tumbledown remnants of the structure and knelt before a gaping gothic arch. Once it had been redolent with Biblical scenes depicted in dazzling stained glass. Now it was just a hole.

The dampness of the grass seeped through the knees of his trousers. He shivered but stayed put. He closed his eyes and put his hands together.

Are you there, Master?

There was no answer. Callum repeated the question, out loud this time.

"I have done your bidding," he said, with a wheedling tone creeping into his voice. "I have done everything you asked of me, and more will I do. But I need to see a sign; I need reassurance from you that I am doing the right thing, that your will is being done."

He opened his eyes. The arch continued to gape, as though in an eternal yawn.

Callum gave up. He got to his feet and brushed off his knees.

"Right," he said. "Fine. I see."

He stomped away, tripping over stones that marked the perimeter of the ruins. He looked quickly over his shoulder to see if anyone – anything – had been watching. Blushing, he headed for home.

As he reached his street, his mood improved. "Well," he reflected, "he didn't exactly tell me to stop, did he?"

He let himself back into the house, not caring how much noise he was making. No more sneaking around! He would continue his present course.

The master would be avenged!

9.

"Two dead men! Two five-pointed stars!" Wheeler's eyes bored into those of each member of her team in turn. They all met her gaze, having learned years ago that to glance away was to invite an attack. "Harry."

"Um..." Harry Henry pushed his glasses up his nose and stumbled to his feet, shedding papers from a folder in the process.

"Jesus squeeze us." Wheeler stepped aside, giving the clumsy detective the floor. He groped in his jacket pockets for a marker pen.

"Um," he said, retrieving one and pulling off the cap. In five surprisingly deft strokes, he reproduced the star design on a flip chart. "The pentagram," he announced. "Also known as the pentacle. An ancient symbol—" he consulted his notes "—approximated by Christians to represent the, um, five wounds of Christ on the cross."

The detectives frowned as they counted off what they could remember of the crucifixion from R.E. lessons... Two in the hands, one in the feet – if the legs were crossed, that is – the crown...

"Hold up!" Stevens interrupted. "Am you telling me it's Christians behind this? A bunch of guitar-strumming, happy-clappy, do-gooders garrotted one man and burned another one alive in his motor? Piss off."

Harry Henry awarded his vulgar colleague a patient smile. "Ah, no; I'm not. Behold!"

He took hold of the flip chart pad and attempted to turn it upside-down, but it got caught on the pegs that attached it to the board. Harry struggled and stumbled. Chief Inspector Wheeler leapt out of the way just as the easel collapsed with Harry Henry on top of it. Stevens laughed like a tickled donkey. Brough and Pattimore helped the hapless Harry to his feet. Brough retrieved the pad and tore off the sheet.

"Is this what you mean?" He turned the page upside-down. The star now had two of its points at the top.

"Yes," said Harry. "An inverted pentacle is a sign of evil."

"Inverted pentacles," scoffed Wheeler. "That'd make you walk funny!"

Miller pointed at the drawing with her biro. "And what way up were they at the murder scenes?"

"The evil way, you dozy bint!" said Wheeler.

"Depends which way you approach it," said Stevens.

"Let's have a look-see," said Wheeler. After some considerable ado, Brough took over her attempts to work the video projector. Images of the crime scenes appeared on the white board. The star on the top of Barry Norwood's car had one point in the direction of the bonnet. The other, beneath the bleeding body of Paul Barker, was apparently the right, non-evil, way up with his head, arms and legs all with a point of their own.

"Interesting," said Pattimore.

"One's good, one's evil," said Wheeler. "What the fuck's going on?"

"Um…" said Harry, wilting under her stare.

"It's like Ben said," Pattimore continued. He approached the screen. "It depends which way you look at it. Here on the car, it's clearly inverted but on the bandstand… if we take the head point to be the bottom – Harry, where are they pointing?"

"Um…"

"What lies in that direction?"

"Um…"

"Get a map," said Brough. Pattimore nodded, glad of the support. "Let's see where they're both pointing."

They set to work at the laptop. A minute later, a Google map appeared on the screen with the locations of the murders pinpointed.

"If we follow a line from the head point of Barker's star, along here…" Brough ran his finger along the white board.

"And another from Norwood's," Pattimore did the same. Their fingers touched. They jumped back, as though electrocuted.

"Priory High School," said Wheeler, squinting at the intersection. "Christ."

"Actually," said Harry, "Christ had nothing to do with it. An inverted pentagram is a symbol of an occult figure called Baphomet. It looks a bit like him, do you see? His horns, his beard – Did I mention he looks like a goat?"

"Fuck off," Wheeler snatched the drawing. "You ain't telling me these men were murdered by an evil goat named Bathmat. Fuck that shit."

"Um, no…" Harry's glasses fell off.

"No, Chief," said Brough. "But his followers…"

Wheeler shook her head. "The only reason to follow a goat is with a bucket and spade. For your roses. Don't give me this devil worship bollocks."

"Lots of nutters out there, Chief," said Stevens.

"They'm not all out there," she shot back. "So, these poor sods each got a star. What else links them? Why them, I mean? Why were they singled out?"

"According to Barker's diary," said Miller, holding out a photocopied sheet, "he was due at a meeting in Birmingham but, of course, he never showed up. On account of being murdered."

"Whoopee-cack," said Wheeler. "So fucking what?"

"The second victim, Barry Norwood, was at that meeting."

Miller's words hung in the air.

"How do you know this, Mel?" said Brough.

Miller smiled. "While you've been running around with my boyfriend, I've been doing my homework."

Brough turned red. "Well, good work, Miller." He cleared his throat.

"And what was this fucking meeting about?" said Wheeler. "Who else was there?"

"Do you think they're at risk, Chief?" said Pattimore.

"I fucking do. I wouldn't be surprised if Bathmat wipes the floor with them."

No one laughed.

"Bunch of bastards," Wheeler snarled. "All right, Brough, Miller, you chase up the missing washing-line. Jason, you take Monkey Man up to the school. I want you in there, undercover."

"How do you mean?" Stevens bristled, correctly surmising that he was the aforementioned Monkey Man. "You want us to dress up as kids?"

Wheeler emitted a hollow laugh. "No, as supply teachers, you dipshit. I want eyes and ears on the floor."

"Can't Brough do it?" Stevens wailed. "He likes dressing up."

"That's true," said Brough, but before he could go on to list the many times he had donned impenetrable disguises in order to bring villains to justice, Wheeler dismissed the option outright.

"Nah. Thanks to his A-list movie star boyfriend, his mug is too well-known. Even if he wore a hat. No, it's got to be you two. Brough, what you can do is try to find where that washing-line came from – you said you had a lead?"

"Yes, Chief."

"Well, put Miler on it and take her for walkies. No offence, Mel; just my little joke."

"What?" said Miller.

"Oh, do try to keep up!"

"No, I get it; I just don't understand why you'm putting Jason and Ben into the school. What's the school got to do with it? Just because some lines on a map…"

Everyone considered Miller's words. She had a point.

"Because I fucking said so," Wheeler snapped. "And because four of those fuckers fucked up the supermarket while I was there! And there's no way they'm getting away with that!"

The team held its collective breath. They knew that when the chief inspector's face turned that particular shade of red, she was not to be contradicted. All they could do was wait until she stopped panting and her shoulders stopped going up and down like twin pistons. Her grip was so tight on a plastic chair that the backrest snapped off.

"Um," Harry Henry dared to speak. "You're bleeding, Chief."

"Yes, too fucking right I'm bleedin' chief and don't you forget it."

"No, I mean literally." He nodded to her hand. Wheeler gaped at it as though it belonged to someone else.

"Coo," said Stevens. "Red blood."

He ducked as the rest of the chair came sailing through the air toward him.

"Harry," said Wheeler, sucking at the wound, "I want more info on the devil worship – anything you can tell me – and also some antiseptic and a plaster." She glared at the team. Blood glistened on her lips. "Go on then," she nodded at the exit. "Fuck off."

***

Stevens's Ford Capri pulled onto the staff car park at Priory High. They had stopped off at Pattimore's flat so that Jason could change into a suit. The only concession Stevens was making was to borrow a tie.

"You'll do, I suppose," was the younger detective's appraisal. "You get some right weirdos as supply teachers."

"And what the fuck's wrong with my tan leather jacket? I've had it for yonks."

"I think you've just answered your own question. Come on."

Pattimore got out, slamming the door more forcefully than Stevens liked.

"Fuck me up a gum tree." Stevens got out and looked at the school. "This is not going to go well."

Pattimore held open the door to Reception. "You must show no fear, Ben. They'll smell it on you."

Stevens whimpered. Chuckling, Pattimore followed him inside.

***

All the curtains were drawn in the Barker house. A sign of mourning, Brough and Miller assumed, not knowing that the Widow Barker was currently living it up at a ski resort with a handsome and virile instructor called Fritz.

It was the house next door that had brought the detectives back to the street. The absence of a washing-line was the only straw they had at which to clutch.

"Looks quiet," Miller observed, locking her car.

"It *sounds* quiet, Miller. Honestly."

"That's what I said. Perhaps they'm asleep."

"Or at work. Or at school."

"One way to find out." Miller pressed the doorbell. Chimes sounded faintly within. They waited. Brough nodded; Miller rang again.

"Nobody's in," she concluded.

"Hmm," said Brough, moving off.

"Where are you going?"

"Around the back," he called over his shoulder.

"Why?"

"Because, Miller, there's bugger all else to do."

In a fluid, athletic move, with his raincoat flapping like a superhero's cape, Brough climbed over the side gate. He unbolted it so Miller could join him.

"I want to have a look at that washing-line."

"Er – there is no washing-line."

"I know. But I'm looking for signs. Was it taken by force? Was it untied?"

"Do you mean, did whoever took it take their time? Indicating it was somebody who lived here – or was it snatched down? Or cut off! By an opportunist!"

"Yes, Miller. Exactly that."

"How will we know?"

"Actually, Miller," Brough looked up and down the Phillipses' back garden, "I haven't a fucking clue."

***

"Sorry, Chief." Harry Henry looked downcast.

"What the fuck for?"

"I haven't got a lollipop to give you and you've been such a brave girl."

"Oh, that's all right, I—" Wheeler stopped herself. "Am you taking the piss?"

"Yes, Chief."

Wheeler made as though to hit him with her newly bandaged hand. Harry, in his capacity as a registered first aider, had done a beautiful job.

"You never fail to surprise me," Wheeler marvelled. "This dressing is better than any I could get down the supermarket."

Harry Henry pushed his wayward spectacles back to their appointed spot. "Don't you mean A and E, Chief?"

"If I'd meant A and E, I would have fucking said A and E. The way this bastard government is going, there'll be no more A and E. It'll be a first aid tent in the supermarket car park; you mark my words."

With this dire prophecy, Chief Inspector Wheeler headed to the door. "You get on with that goat thing, chicken. It occurs to me there's somebody I need to phone."

"Oh?" Harry blinked, his eyes magnified by his prescription lenses. "Who are you going to call?"

Wheeler smiled grimly. "CostBusters."

***

From the far end of the garden, Brough called to Miller who was on the patio under the kitchen window. "Can you see anything?"

"I can't," said Miller. She jumped on the spot, craning her neck. "There's a hook or something; the line could have gone through there."

"There's another one here," said Brough, "a hook on the shed. Although that would have meant the line was hanging rather low. I wouldn't want to dry my sheets on it, I can tell you."

"I don't want to know about your wet sheets," Miller grumbled. She pointed at the path. "Prop."

"I beg your pardon."

"Line prop," she pointed again. "You use them to prop the line up."

"No shit."

"Keeps your sheets off the ground."

Brough came toward her. Lying alongside the path was a long, wooden pole with a cleft at the end.

"Well spotted, Miller. Props to you."

"Give it a rest, sir," Miller scowled.

"No, this is very interesting actually, Miller. This prop indicated that this household was at one time in possession of a washing-line."

"Fascinating."

Brough's enthusiasm waned. "Oh, what are we doing, Miller? Prancing around like – like—"

"Fairies at the bottom of the garden, sir?"

Brough narrowed his eyes. "I mean, there's a juicy double homicide and we're footling around on a wild goose chase."

"It *is* the murder weapon, sir," Miller pointed out.

"Well, yes…" He kicked at a stray piece of gravel.

"In this job, you've got to take the boring with the exciting. You know that, sir."

"Well, yes… Oh, stop being so bloody reasonable, Miller. Let's go and submit our report. Write this down: there was a washing-line here but now there isn't. Did you get all that?"

But Miller wasn't listening. She was peering in at the French windows that opened into the living room, her hands cupped around the sides of her head. "Um, sir…"

"What now? Don't tell me they hang their clothes up indoors."

"No, sir. Not their clothes."

"What do you mean? Stop talking in bloody riddles."

He pressed his forehead against the glass and squinted into the darkened room.

A woman was suspended from the light fitting. Her feet hovered over a pentagram sketched on the carpet in charcoal.

"Mrs Phillips, do you think?"

"Probably, sir. Better make that a triple homicide."

***

"At fucking last! It'd be easier to get a sniff at the Pope's ring piece than to get you to answer your fucking phone."

Dennis Lord laughed with delight. "Karen fucking Wheeler! I'd recognise those dulcet fucking tones any-fucking-where. It's been a long time."

"Not fucking long enough. Listen, shit stain, I want you to come in."

"Come in where? Your fanny?"

"I wouldn't let you touch my fanny even if you had a ten-foot pole. Which, if memory serves, you don't. Get your scabby arse down to Dedley nick at once."

"I shall do no such fucking thing."

"I'll send a car."

"You'll do no such fucking thing. It's impossible, Karen. I'm a very busy man."

"It's not an invitation to a fucking cream tea, Dennis."

Dennis Lord stopped spinning in his chair, catching the edge to Wheeler's voice. "You'm serious."

"Of course I'm fucking serious. Do you honestly think I'd make a social call – to you, of all bastards?"

"Well, um, no. I suppose not. What's this all about, Karen?"

"We have reason to believe you may be a target. It may have escaped your notice but two people to whom you have connections have recently been slaughtered. A Paul Barker and a Barry Norwood."

Dennis sat up straight. His eyes darted in all directions as if any number of maniacs might be hiding in his office. His throat was suddenly parched. Wheeler had used the word 'slaughtered'. Not 'killed' or 'murdered' but 'slaughtered'…

"Now…" he tried to laugh. "Why would anyone possibly want to kill me?"

Wheeler's laughter was more convincing. "You know and I know you'm only still above ground level because I'm able to exercise fucking restraint. Listen, you stubborn twat. Come to the nick. Bring your laptop, your phone, your fucking teddy bear if you have to, but I need you under police protection."

"Why, Karen! I'm touched!"

"Not by me you won't be."

"Look, it's sweet of you to think of me but it's really out of the question. My schedule is tight – certainly tighter than your flappy old minge. I just can't get away. In fact, I'm due at the Dedley hyperstore in half an hour."

"Oh, really?" Wheeler's cogs turned and clicked. "Then I think I've come up with a compromise."

"Oh? Really?"

"Yes," Karen Wheeler grinned to herself. "I'm going to assign you two of my best men. They'll stick to you like shit to a blanket and you, Dennis my love, can go wherever the fuck you want. Their names are Wren and Hobley and they'll meet you at your fucking shop."

She disconnected. I've done my bit, she smiled to herself. I've arranged protection – of sorts.

It was no more or no less than that bastard Dennis Lord deserved.

***

Pattimore discovered Stevens in the male staff toilets. The detective inspector was splashing water on his face. Drops clung to the thick bristles of his porn star moustache.

"Jesus…" was Stevens's acknowledgment of his partner's presence. While Pattimore used a urinal, Stevens continued to sigh and swear until the detective constable looked over his shoulder.

"Something wrong, Ben?"

"Gold star for the detective with his dick in his hand," Stevens snarled. "Have you seen the state of this place? It's a fucking warzone."

"Is it?" Pattimore shook himself and zipped up. He joined Stevens at the washbasins. In the mirror, Stevens looked more haggard than usual.

"Year 8 Maths not go well, then?"

"Well? Well?! I've never seen such fucking savagery. I just about escaped with my fucking life. Monsters, the lot of them. I thought I'd wandered into the fucking zoo by mistake and there'd been an outbreak of rabies. It ain't funny."

Pattimore barely tried to suppress his smirk. He squirted a dollop of foam onto his hands and washed it off. "I had Year 10 for Textiles. They were as good as gold."

"Textiles? What's that? Fucking sewing! Right up your alley."

The bell signalled the end of break. Stevens whimpered.

"Any signs of the hooded hoodlums?"

"Who? Snap, Crackle and Wank? No. I was too busy dodging paper darts and furniture."

Stevens's phone rang. The theme tune to *Starsky and Hutch* echoed around the tiled room.

"Hello?" He listened. "Fucking hell. Who?… Right you are. Cheers."

He pocketed the phone.

"Well?"

"Looks like we've got a Get Out of Hell card. That was your old bum chum."

Pattimore winced at the reference to his former relationship with D I Brough. Stevens observed the flinch and enjoyed it.

"There's been another one. Some woman. Her kid goes to this school. We've got to find him and tell him."

"Shit," said Pattimore. "Poor kid."

"Be like looking for a needle in a mountain of shit in this place."

"Don't be stupid," Pattimore snapped. "He'll be timetabled, won't he? We can find out which class he's in and go and get him."

"Oh, yeah. That didn't work with the other three, did it? Larry, Curly and Fuckwit."

"Inveterate truants, that deputy called them. But this kid—"

"Callum Phillips."

"—should be easier to track down. Come on. Dry your eyes and we'll go and ask the school secretary to reveal his whereabouts."

"I wasn't actually crying, you prick," Stevens assured him as they walked along the corridor to the school office. "It's just that a paper dart caught me right there."

"Yes, Ben," said Pattimore. "Now, work your charms on the secretary and get the information we need. What am I saying? Just show her your i.d."

***

But Callum Phillips was absent from the Science lesson where the timetable predicted he would be. The teacher, a wild-haired, bespectacled agglomeration of wrinkles and skin tags, shook his head sadly.

"Such a good boy. Top of the class. Off the charts. But lately, he's been distracted. Absent-minded. And now, absent-bodied too. Sad when they go off the boil like that."

"So, you'm telling me you've no fucking clue where he might be?" Stevens grumbled in a harsh whisper. Pattimore bundled his colleague from the lab.

"It's a school, Ben, not a prison."

"Prison's too fucking good for them."

Pattimore stared at him. "I've never seen you this rattled. What did they do to you?"

"I don't want to talk about it."

Pattimore tried not to laugh. He gave Stevens a mock pat on the back to console him, deftly removing a sheet of paper he found taped between the detective inspector's shoulder blades.

CUNT, it said.

"Hoi! What are you doing?" Stevens reached behind his back. Pattimore showed him the paper. "Oh, that. I put that there. To show them I'm not one to be messed with."

"Oh, really?" Pattimore scoffed. "Worked like a charm, did it?"

He balled the paper and bounced it off Stevens's forehead. "Come on. We need to find this Phillips kid. Let's hope he's easier to track down than that bloody zorilla."

"I doubt he'll leave a trail of his own shit. He's probably gone home."

"I doubt it."

"Why?"

"Well, Brough's at his house, isn't he? Along with the team

investigating the scene of the boy's mother's murder."

"Not with you…"

"Davey wouldn't have phoned us if the boy was with him, would he?"

"Oh. Suppose not."

"You need to get your head in the game, Ben. Come on – and before you say 'pub', we're getting a coffee."

***

"This is most inconvenient, I'll have you know."

Beatrice Mooney was displeased, to put it mildly. She glared across the table at the mild-mannered detective with the insipid smile. He had an irritating habit of pushing his spectacles up his nose every few seconds. Why didn't he buy a pair that bloody fit him?

"Sugar?" smiled Harry Henry.

"I beg your pardon."

Harry nodded at the tea tray between them. At Dedley nick there was no room for vending machines. "In your tea. I'll be mother."

"My mother would never have detained me against my will," Beatrice Mooney pouted. "It's outrageous. You should be locking up the criminals! Poor Paul's killer for one!"

Harry glanced over his shoulder as though to check something. "The door isn't locked."

"Then I am free to leave?"

"If you want. Free to go out into a town where there's somebody who wants to kill you."

"Ridiculous! You're barking mad!"

"Am I? Barker wouldn't think me barking mad. Nor would Norwood." Harry clasped his hands together and leaned toward the head teacher. "I understand you're keen to get back to the classroom, Ms Mooney, but—"

She cut him off with a hollow laugh.

"Now you *are* being ridiculous! I don't have a classroom, Inspector Henry. I don't face the children! I'm an administrator!"

She pronounced the word with immense pride. Harry Henry was unimpressed.

"All the same, if you want to get back to – whatever it is you do, you have to help us with our enquiries."

"I don't see what I could poss—"

"Ms Mooney, think! Is there anyone you have crossed recently? Anyone at all?"

Beatrice Mooney shook her head. She pouted.

"Anyone who might want Paul Barker dead? Barry Norwood? Dennis Lord?"

Her face paled. "Dennis isn't – is he?"

"No! No! He's under police protection too."

"Is he here? May I see him?"

"No… he's at work. He has been assigned a couple of officers—"

Beatrice Mooney slapped the table, making the tea service rattle. "That's what I want! Assign me some bodyguards! Let me get back to work!"

"Um…" Harry Henry was thrown. He pushed his glasses up his nose. "I'm not sure that's…"

Beatrice Mooney sat back and crossed her arms. She arched an eyebrow. Harry Henry capitulated. He bumbled to his feet; his chair scraped the floor.

"I'll see what the boss—" he gestured at the door before waddling through it.

"Jesus…" Beatrice Mooney scowled. Alone in the interview room, her nerve failed her. The detective's questions echoed in her mind.

Who would want to kill you?

Who would want to kill Paul? And Barry?

Why is Dennis under police protection?

She chewed at her lip. It had to be the sponsorship proposal. That was the only thing that connected her to the victims and the victims to each other.

But the plans were still very much a secret. If she revealed them – if word got out – there could be an outcry. Corruption! Backhanders!

Those bloody Lefties, banging on about education being a right...

Then again, if she told that clumsy fool of a detective, it could lead to a swift resolution – an arrest!

Now, who would be most vehemently opposed to Priory High becoming CostBusters Academy?

Harry Henry crashed back into the room. "Um," he said. "We don't really have the man- or woman-power to give you a couple of bodyguards, Ms, but—"

He made calming gestures to pre-empt an outburst. "The Chief says you can go back to school, provided I go with you."

"Good," Beatrice Mooney said coldly. She got to her feet. "And when you get there you can arrest the deputy head."

10.

At lunchtime, a fight broke out on the playing field. Kids poured from the dining hall and filled the embankment, bloodthirsty spectators in a Roman arena. The gladiators grappling on the grass were Logger and Callum. They swung their arms at each other, shoving and grabbing, while the crowd chanted, "Fight! Fight!" in case anyone was in any doubt about what was going on.

Stevens and Pattimore joined the exodus, catching up with and overtaking a couple of on-duty teachers who seemed in no particular hurry to break up the fray.

"Leave them a bit," advised the Science teacher they had met earlier. "That Logan Lawrence deserves a good kicking."

Pattimore pointed at the pugilistic pair. "Which one's Logan Lawrence?"

The Science teacher winced; the crowd cheered. "That one who's just landed on his nose."

Pattimore bounded to the battling boys.

"Who's the other one?" said Stevens with the air of a man about to place a bet on the victor. The Science teacher squinted through his spectacles.

"My word! I didn't recognise him without his glasses. The boy giving Logger a pasting is Callum Phillips. Well, well! I never knew he had it in him."

"Shit!" Stevens hurried to catch up with Pattimore.

Logger was back on his feet. He rushed the specky (temporarily spec-less) twat, ramming his head against Callum's sternum. Callum staggered back and then brought up his knee under Logger's jaw. The crowd roared in approval.

Pattimore jogged up. "Boys! Boys! That's enough of that."

Logger froze, distracted. Callum head-butted him on the forehead. Logger dropped onto his backside. Pattimore stood over him; by the time Stevens arrived, Callum had run away, through the bushes and out through the gap in the fence.

"Shit," Stevens panted, leaning forward with his hands on his thighs. "You know who that was?"

"Who?" said Pattimore. He offered a hand to the boy on the ground. Logger scowled, declining assistance. Dogger and Bonk stepped forward, proffering his coat and bag; Logger glowered at them as well.

"Only Callum whatsit," said Stevens, staring at the hedges.

"Shit," said Pattimore.

"He fucking started it, sir," said Logger, stating the case for his own defence.

"Yeah, yeah," said Pattimore. He showed Logger his i.d. The boy paled. "You can tell me all about it indoors."

He and Stevens frogmarched Logger up the concrete steps, through the crowd and into the main building. Someone recognised the supply teacher with the porn-star moustache and within seconds a new chant arose.

"Mis-ter Cunt! Mis-ter Cunt!"

Stevens couldn't get inside fast enough.

***

Brough and Miller were invited to wait on the garden path while the crime scene investigation unit… investigated the scene of the crime. Brough paced, impatient, while Miller was more philosophical.

"They don't want us getting under their feet," she said. "In case we touch something."

"I don't know about you, Miller," Brough sneered, "but I'm a trained professional. I wasn't planning on running around the place like a two-year old."

"No," Miller muttered. "You'm just sulking like one."

"What was that?"

"Nothing. Sir."

Miller was spared a grilling by the emergence of the SOCO through the patio doors.

"Well?" Brough rounded on him. The SOCO glanced at Miller, who both shrugged and smiled helplessly.

"Oh, she's dead all right," said the SOCO, "if that's what you've been waiting to hear."

"Ha!" said Brough.

"He's not in the mood," said Miller. "Anything else you can tell us?"

"It looks like death by hanging – I doubt it's suicide, given the – well – I'll call it 'staging', for want of a better word. The use of a clothes line, and that five-pointed star, of course."

"This death is linked to the others, then?" Brough said in even tones, mastering his temper – he was, after all, a trained professional.

"On the face of it, yes."

"You sound doubtful," Miller observed.

"It's the same star, all right," the SOCO shook his head, "And, again, we'd have to run tests: graphology and the like…"

"But…" Brough and Miller prompted him in unison.

"But…" said the SOCO, "I'd be willing to bet this star was not made by the same person who did the other two."

***

In the absence of the head teacher, Pattimore and Stevens commandeered her office for the purposes of questioning the boy Logan Lawrence, also known as Logger.

"I can't believe this," the youth held a ball of tissues to his bloodied nose. "There's murders going on and you'm picking on me about mucking about in a supermarket."

"Murders?" said Stevens, as though trying out the word for the first time. "What's a scrote like you know about the murders?"

"It's all over the telly, ain't it?" said Logger. "Or ain't you got one in your cave?"

"Cheeky bastard. You won't be so cheeky in a minute when I charge you with wilful damage."

Logger's smirk did not falter. "You can't prove nothing."

"Oh, no?" said Pattimore, perching a buttock on Beatrice Mooney's desk. "There's CCTV. You've been identified as one of the youths involved."

"Bollocks. Who? Who told you that?"

"Never you mind. A trustworthy source."

"Who?"

"Listen, Logan – *Logger*," Pattimore smiled. "Give us the names of the other boys and things will go easy for you."

"I ain't no grass! Besides, I weren't even there."

"We'll be talking to your friends," said Stevens, checking his notebook. "Doggo and... Blink, is that? My handwriting!"

"Dogger and Bonk!" said Logger.

"So you admit they were with you!"

"Yes! No! You'm trying to trick me!" Logger wiped his sweaty palms on his thighs. "They was with me, all right. But not at Costbosters. Nowhere near."

"We never mentioned the name of the supermarket." It was Stevens's turn to smirk.

"Shit," said Logger.

"So, who was the fourth one?" said Pattimore. "Was it your friend? Callum?"

Logger sneered. "That wanker."

"What was that fight about?"

"What fight?"

"The one you just had with Callum Phillips."

"Nothing," Logger shrugged.

100

"I'd hate to see it when you fall out over something!" said Pattimore.

"I'd love to see it," said Stevens. "I'd bring popcorn."

"He's a weirdo," Logger folded his arms. "Proper fucking nerd. And he rocks up and tries to take over. Like he's the one in charge. Well, he ain't. I'm the one in charge. What I say goes."

"He looked to be in charge to me," said Stevens. "He knocked seven shades of shit out of you."

"I was just getting warmed up, wasn't I?" said Logger, defensively. "I was going to kill him—" he caught himself, "—Well, not actually *kill him* kill him – but you know. Show him who's boss."

"Fine way to carry on," Stevens tutted. "When that poor lad's going through terrible tragedy—"

"Ben!" Pattimore warned.

"What?" said Logger.

"His poor old mother," said Stevens. "Terrible."

"What do you mean? What's happened?"

"That's enough!" Pattimore bundled Stevens from the room. "What the fuck are you playing at?"

Stevens laughed. "Did you see his face? He hasn't a clue about the murders."

"Nobody said he would have. Wheeler wants him done for the supermarket vandalism."

"Well, at least we can rule him out of the murders."

"Fuck sake, Ben."

"Is there a problem, gentlemen?"

The detectives turned to find Deputy Head Alfred Abbott regarding them with annoyance. "For how much longer are you going to cause disruption in my school?"

Stevens drew himself up to his full height. "Long as it takes, sunshine."

"I am sure the Head will have something to say when she finds you using her office."

"You're right, Alfred," said Beatrice Mooney, her high heels clicking as she approached. Harry Henry lumbered along behind her, carrying her bags.

"All right, Harry!" Stevens grinned, raising his hand for a high-five that he didn't get. "Come to join the party?"

"Um…" said Harry Henry, his glasses askew.

"There's the man I was telling you about," Beatrice Mooney extended a manicured finger in Mr Abbott's direction. "Take him away!"

"Um," said Harry.

The three detectives looked at each other and from head teacher to deputy and back again.

"Go on!" Beatrice Mooney flapped her hand. "There's your murderer!"

"Oh, well, in that case…" Stevens pulled handcuffs from his jacket.

"You would not dare," said Mr Abbott.

Stevens dared.

***

Callum ran from the school field to the ruined priory. He loitered among the crumbling walls, desperate to learn what his next move should be.

Where are you, he agonised? Where the bloody hell are you?

He addressed the question to the great arch window as if expecting the Goat Man to appear.

He didn't.

Perhaps it was too early. Too light.

On the previous occasions, it had been dark. The middle of the night. In the garden.

And the first time – the first time, out on the field, crouching in those bushes, while those three idiots giggled on the steps, Callum hadn't seen anything at all.

But he had heard.

Don't turn around!

Callum had heard that all right.

Don't turn around, Callum Phillips.

"Who are you?"

I am your master. You will do my bidding and those who cross me shall perish.

"Oh?" said Callum. "Who's that, then?"

You shall know. And soon. First, I must have your allegiance.

"Um…"

Do you not wish to be strong? To conquer those who torment you?

"Well, I…"

I shall show you the way.

"I don't know…"

Serve me and you shall never be bullied again.

"Well, I – oh, all right then. I'm in. But—"

Do not turn around. Your neighbour.

"Mr Barker?"

Yes. He.

And so it had happened. Callum had enticed his neighbour to the park. Mr Barker had lain on the bandstand disturbingly readily, paying no attention to the five-pointed star – perhaps he'd thought it was just graffiti.

"Kinky, eh?" he had chuckled when Callum had produced the washing-line.

They were Paul Barker's last words.

11.

With the body removed and the forensic team packed up and gone, Brough and Miller had the whole house to go over.

"What am we looking for, exactly?" said Miller, following Brough up the stairs to the bedrooms.

"Clues, Miller. You might have heard of such things. Essential in our profession."

He moved along the landing but Miller remained at the top of the stairs. "All right," she said. "What's this all in aid of?"

"Solving a murder. Three murders."

"Not this. That," she pointed at his head and her finger described a circle. "Your mardy face. You've been in a right old grump for days."

"I have not!"

"You have! You've got a face like a bulldog's arsehole."

"I don't think that's the expression, Miller."

"I don't give a monkey's toss. Something's crawled up your bum and died. You can talk to me, you know."

"As ever, Miller, your sensitivity is overwhelming. But let's keep our minds on the job, shall we?"

He opened a door. The master bedroom. All floral prints and wicker.

"Ugh," said Brough in the doorway.

"Bed's not made," said Miller, peering around him.

"Well, I think we can forgive a little slovenliness, Miller, since the woman's been murdered."

"Not what I mean," Miller pushed past him. "Do you see? Only one side has been slept in. Where was the husband last night?"

"He works away."

"Or plays away? Eh? Think about it."

"Do I have to?"

"Hubby says he's working away. Perfect alibi. Nips back, hangs the wife in the style of murders that are currently the fad. Leaves him free to be with his bit on the side."

Miller looked exceedingly pleased with herself. Brough scowled.

"You should write shit novels for the internet, Miller. Clog up people's kindles with your nonsense; I don't want to hear it. We need to contact Mr Phillips. Contrary to your hypothesis, he may not be aware of his wife's death."

Miller pouted, crestfallen. "And the son? We need to tell him as well."

Brough hummed in agreement. "I doubt Jason and that wanker Stevens will have tracked him down at the school. Someone will have to wait here in case he shows up."

"As long as that someone's not me," said Miller. "I need to get home. Darren's moving in tonight."

"Moving in?" Brough shuddered at the thought. "Spare me the details, please."

"To the flat, I mean. Makes sense. Financially. Silly to keep toothbrushes in two different places."

"Well, if you put it like that. But are you sure, Mel?"

Miller frowned. "I know my track record with men is worse than the bubonic plague's, but Darren's a good one. The best. It makes sense to take our relationship to the next level."

"You make it sound like a video game. Anyway, remember when I said we should keep our minds on the job?"

He tried another door.

"Poo," Miller cried. "It stinks."

Callum's bedroom bore all the hallmarks of the teenager's lair. Posters of footballers and pop starlets vied for prominence. A desk groaned under the weight of school books. A model aeroplane, dusty and neglected, hung from the ceiling. The floor was covered with discarded clothes and abandoned and forgotten dinner plates.

"Sweaty socks and mouldy pizza crusts," Miller fanned her nose with her hand. "And I dread to think what else besides! Teenage boys! You must remember what that was like."

"What?"

"I assume you were one once. A teenage boy."

"What are you on about, Miller?"

"Of course, that was a long time ago," she shrugged. "A long, long time ago."

Brough glowered at her, Caesar betrayed by Brutus.

"Focus, Miller. Any clues – where might he go? After-school clubs? Friends' names? Anything at all."

"Well, I'm not looking under the bed," said Miller. "You can go through the crusty tissues; I'll have a look over here."

She busied herself with Callum's desk, his school books and set texts. Brough steeled himself and lifted a corner of the duvet.

"Well, well!" cried Miller, making him jump. "I don't think he's doing this for GCSE, do you?"

She held up a book so Brough could read the title.

"*A History of the Occult in the Black Country…*" Brough took it from her and thumbed through it. "Look, Miller. Those five-pointed stars."

"That ain't the half of it," said Miller, pointing at the spine. "Look who wrote it."

Brough turned the book over and read the author's name. "Donald Phillips…"

"It's him, isn't it?" Miller grinned, smugly. "The husband!"

***

"This really is a most egregious mistake."

Stevens folded his arms and looked across the table at the red-faced deputy head. "That's what they all fucking say. Granted, most of them don't use big words like – what was it, gregarious? – but the gist is the same."

Alfred Abbott's cheeks reddened. He folded his arms too but his posture lacked Stevens's slouch.

Pattimore slid a sheet of paper toward the interviewee. "Do you recognise this?"

Abbott barely glanced at it. "It's a sheet of paper. Like countless others."

"Are you able to identify it?"

"White, A4. Standard photocopier fodder."

Stevens grunted. "Smart arse."

"Not the paper, Mr Abbott; what's on it."

"You really should be more precise in your questioning," Abbott smirked. He pulled the paper toward him and glanced at the image on it. "It's a five-pointed star. A pentagram or pentacle."

The detectives looked at each other.

"Come across many of these in your line of work?" Stevens scoffed.

"Not on a daily basis, no."

"But you were able to identify it right away," said Pattimore.

"My dear sir, I can identify many things. It is one of the benefits of a good education."

"And does that education involve dabbling in the occult?"

Abbott laughed. "Is that a serious question, Detective Constable?"

"This is a serious investigation," said Stevens. "Two men are dead."

"And a woman," added Pattimore. "Designs like this were found at each scene."

"And so you think, because I can put a name to it, I must be responsible. That's something of a stretch, don't you think?"

The detectives looked at each other again: an unspoken handing over of the reins. Stevens sat up.

"Where'd you go to school? Somewhere posh?"

"Hardly," Abbott frowned. "As I told you previously, I went to Priory High. Except it was not known by that name back then."

"The Grammar?"

Abbott let out a bitter laugh. "Sadly, alas, no. By the time I got there, the grammar school days were over. Actually, I was one of the first intake the year Dedley Grammar became The Dedley School – an astounding lack of imagination on the part of the people who name schools, I must say."

"You seem – remorseful – is that the word?"

"Resentful, I think you'll find. Do you know, I was! I was altogether convinced I would have passed the Eleven Plus examination and earned my place among the grammar school boys. I suppose I resented missing the chance to prove my mettle. I mean, after all, *anyone* can get into a comprehensive."

He pronounced this last word with a visible grimace of distaste. He watched Pattimore make a note.

"But this is ancient history; what has any of this to do with your murder investigations?"

"We'll get there," said Stevens. "Hold your fucking horses." He grinned to see the educator bristle at his bad language. "We'll fucking get there all fucking right."

Abbott's lip curled. "Then I wish you would get a fucking move on."

Stevens was gobsmacked. "A teacher! Swearing! Just wait until I tell the lads at playtime."

"You work in the same school you went to," Pattimore observed. "Bit weird, isn't it?"

"How so? Perhaps at first. Some of the old masters were still there – and I had thought them ancient when I was their pupil! To have them as colleagues was a little strange, I admit. Those old grammar school buffers insisting I call them Roger or Martin. They would always be 'Sir' to me. They became my mentors. Got me through my first year. The school may have changed, they said, there may be girls here now, but there is no reason to let standards slip. We may be a comprehensive school now but there is no reason why we should not be the best damned comprehensive in the borough."

Pattimore scribbled further notes. "So, Dedley Grammar became the Dedley School but now it's called Priory High. When did that happen?"

"In 1989."

"Why?" said Stevens.

Abbott looked downcast. "Despite our best efforts, the school was failing. The old grammar staff were all retired or dead or both. We were slipping in the league tables. The school was put into so-called special measures and rebranded as a 'specialist Science college'. We got a new Science block out of it but little else."

"But you stayed?" said Pattimore. "You didn't move to a better job in a better school."

"Young man, one does not abandon one's preferred football team when it goes through a rocky patch. There is such a thing as loyalty."

Pattimore nodded.

"So," said Stevens. "What do you think about the school's impending academy status? Does that piss you off?"

Abbott's lip curled. "Academia has nothing to do with it."

"You don't sound too happy about that."

"No one who cares a jot for education would. They don't work. Well, not in the interests of the students."

"In whose interests do they work, then?"

Abbott tapped the side of his nose. "Follow the money, Detective Constable."

At that moment, Chief Inspector Wheeler burst in.

"Hoi, Bobbsy Twins! A word." She burst out again.

"Excuse us." Pattimore got to his feet. Stevens followed him to the corridor where Wheeler was waiting. She had been listening in and was far from happy.

"What the fuck is all this shit?" she gestured angrily at the interview room door. "I don't want his fucking C.V. or a history of education in the fucking town. Pin him down on the fucking star thing."

"I'm leading up to it," said Pattimore.

"We got him to swear," boasted Stevens. "He said fuck."

"Then let's throw the fucking key away. Think! Why would a man of his experience be against this academy business? Eh?"

"Um... he sees it as a decline in standards..." Pattimore grasped for ideas.

"And that might lead him to kill? Three people? I fucking doubt it. Think! He's spent most of his life in that place, man and boy – although not necessarily in that fucking order."

"His job!" Stevens cried. "He thinks he's going to lose his job!"

"Hooray!" Wheeler applauded. "I've been boning up – don't snigger! These academies are notorious for getting shot of their most senior staff."

"Why?" said Pattimore.

"Like he said," Wheeler nodded at the door, "Follow the money. Senior staff are expensive. Much cheaper to get somebody fresh out of training."

"Is it enough?" said Pattimore. "Enough to turn him into a killer?"

"That's what we have to establish," said Wheeler. "Let's hang on to the fucker for a bit. Check his whereabouts at the times of the murders. Seems to me that school has been his entire life. He just might resent being elbowed out of it – And what the fuck are you giggling at, you lanky wanker?"

Stevens wiped his eyes and pressed an arm against his aching ribs. "He said fuck."

"Get him talking about the star," Wheeler directed her instructions to Pattimore. "What can he tell us – might prove useful – Also, how does he know? He might let something slip."

"Yes, Chief."

"Give that lanky wanker a minute to pull himself together then get back in there. I'm warning you, Stevens: grow up or I'll kick you so hard your bollocks will come out of your fucking nose."

She strode away.

"Have you finished?" Pattimore sighed.

Tight-lipped, Stevens nodded. Then a snort escaped him and he was off again.

***

"I like what you've done with the place." Brough was standing in Miller's living room. "Looks like an explosion in a sports shop."

"It's Darren's," Miller called from the kitchen. "Coffee?"

"Mineral water, if you have it," Brough called back.

"You can have tap and like it." Miller joined him while the kettle boiled. She looked around at the heaps of tracksuits and exercise equipment. "It's only temporary. He had to give up his lock-up. Damp, apparently."

"Hm," said Brough. Using his finger and thumb as pincers, he removed a jockstrap from the sofa so he could sit down. "Are you sure he's not taking advantage of you, Mel?"

Miller hooted. "Every night and weekend mornings." She laughed to see Brough shudder.

"You must be getting serious."

Miller grinned. "We'm on the right track, yes. It's nice to have somebody I can trust and who trusts me, you know? Darren's a keeper – and I don't mean up at the zoo. And I'd still got some money left after I sold my mom's house, so…"

"Miller…" Brough growled. "What have you done?"

"It's just a loan! He'll pay it back; I know he will."

Brough sighed and shook his head. "Oh, Miller. How much?"

"That's none of your—"

"How much?"

"Ten."

"Pounds."

"Yes. Ten thousand of them."

Brough was aghast. "Oh, Mel; you haven't known him for five minutes. You won't see that money again."

"You don't know that! You don't know him like I do." Tears sprang to Miller's eyes. Brough was just jealous – she didn't want to believe he might be right.

Brough gave up. "Just make the drinks, Miller and then try Donald Phillips again."

"I've left oodles of messages." Miller composed herself.

"Leave oodles more."

"Yes, sir." She withdrew to the kitchen. Brough's phone rattled in his pocket. A video call was coming through. From Oscar.

"Hey!" the film star's voice crackled. The image on screen froze and juddered. "David! Hope this is a good time – Can you see me?"

"Yes," said Brough, keeping his voice low in case Miller was earwigging. "I thought we were doing this later."

The famous lips pouted. "That's just it, baby. Later's no good for me. Got to do a whole bunch of reshoots. We're behind schedule big time."

Brough groaned; he guessed what was coming. "No," he said.

"Afraid so, baby. I'm not going to make it over for your big day."

"No!" Brough snapped. "Don't say it!"

"But…" Oscar flashed his toothy grin and wiggled his eyebrows. "I do have an alternative…" He waved an envelope at his webcam. It filled the screen but was too out of focus for Brough to read.

"Is that…"

"I'll get it couriered over right away, sweet cheeks. In plenty of time for your big day. Now, I gotta go." He blew a kiss. "Bye, baby."

The call disconnected. Brough became aware that Miller was standing in the doorway with a mug of tea and a glass of tap water. He blushed.

"Oscar?" she asked, affecting innocence. Brough nodded curtly and put his phone away. "All right, is he?"

"He's…well, you know… busy."

"That's show business, I suppose." She offered him the glass. "Must be hard."

Brough crossed his legs.

"Being apart so much, I mean." She perched on the arm of an armchair that was currently accommodating a huge, silver exercise ball and a tangle of skipping ropes. "At least my Darren's within reach."

"Well, his stuff is," sneered Brough. "Keep trying to get Phillips."

He got to his feet and handed back the glass of water. "Bathroom through here?"

"Take a left at the exercise bike and mind the rowing-machine."

"Honestly, Miller…" Brough picked his way out of the room as though traversing a minefield. Miller poked her tongue out at his back.

"Honestly, sweet cheeks," she grumbled.

12.

Alfred Abbott settled back in his chair. "Actually, it's something of a coincidence."

"What is?" said Stevens.

"All this business with the pentagrams."

"This business, as you put it," said Pattimore, "is the murder of three individuals."

"Quite. I am not being dismissive. I just find it curious that the stars are appearing now, right at the time when I am about to launch my blog."

"What blog?" said Stevens.

"I have written, gentlemen, the definitive history of the school. Alas, so far I have been unable to arouse the interest of a publisher."

"You don't fucking say," said Stevens. Abbott ignored him.

"And so, rather than taking the vanity route and publishing the book myself, I am putting it out there, into the ether, so that it might attract a global audience. When I approach the publishers with the figures – how many 'hits' I'm getting, as I believe the phrasing is, they will be falling over themselves to make me a deal."

There was a light in his eyes, a mixture of passion and delusion – and perhaps pound signs too. Pattimore and Stevens exchanged sidelong glances.

"Go on, then," said Pattimore. "Tell us. Tell us why the stars are so important to the school."

Alfred Abbott pursed his lips. He relished the opportunity to speak of his favourite subject.

"Are you sitting comfortably, gentlemen?"

"Oh, just fucking get on with it," said Stevens.

***

The school was founded in the middle of the sixteenth century in a modest, wooden hut on the hill overlooking the priory. Up until then, the education of the town's boys had been the preserve of the resident religious order, who selected the sons of the well-to-do – boys who were never destined to toil in the fields or to scrape a living from the open-cast mines. Some of the boys stayed on, taking holy orders while others furthered their studies at university.

But then, Henry VIII decreed that monasteries, abbeys and indeed priories were to be disbanded and in most cases demolished. The prior at the time submitted an appeal, a stay of execution, if you will. He argued that the building should be allowed to stand and his order to continue its important work as educators.

It might have worked, were it not for the emergence of one man, one Baxter Emmanuel, ironically himself a former student of the priory. Freshly returned from Oxford and a grand tour of Europe, he saw which way the wind was blowing and built his hut on land leased from the Earl of Dedley. With his new-fangled, puritanical ways, he lured the sons of the merchants away from the priory with the promise that there was no risk of the boys ending up as monks or friars. He would educate them in the ways of the world and in commerce – especially commerce.

The intake grew. The hut was extended, then rebuilt in brick and stone. Meanwhile, at the foot of the hill, the priory was being sacked and looted and its inhabitants driven out. The prior went to see the headmaster and pleaded for employment. He had the knowledge, he argued, the skills and the expertise, to be a valuable addition to the teaching staff.

"And will you renounce your robes?" Baxter Emmanuel asked. "Will you forsake your papist ways?"

"Aye," said the prior. "For we have never been an ostentatious order. Living frugal lives and eschewing the pomp and ceremony of high church."

For a time, it worked. The former prior taught the boys Latin and penmanship while the status of the headmaster grew around the town and beyond.

Rather than pay fees for their sons' education, the merchants were encouraged to make donations to the school fund. Seeing the headmaster parade around in cloth of gold and ermine, the former prior began to suspect that not all of the school fund was being spent on the building or on the boys.

Matters came to a head – so to speak – when the Latin master petitioned for new thatch for the roof of his classroom.

"There simply is not the money," Baxter Emmanuel sighed. "What funds we have are spent on teaching the boys. Now, if you were to agree to a reduction in salary..."

"You mean pay for the roof myself!"

"It would be in the interests of school spirit."

"Good day to you, Headmaster."

The Latin master stormed from the school. His angry strides took him to the recently ruined priory, where he fell to his knees and wept. Once he had had direction in his life, and purpose. Serve God and civilise the boys of Dedley so that they too might serve the Lord. As prior, he had been a stone dropped in a pond and his work the ripples, stretching out, reaching farther and farther. But now that pond was stagnating – or something of that nature – he had not fully realised his metaphor.

He reached inside his shirt of coarse cloth and closed his fist around his wooden crucifix.

"I have done nothing but in service of thee," he spat, "and you bring me down thusly. Each man must have his trials – this much I know – but that, that hypocrite would surely drive Job to distraction and dark thoughts of – of..."

His voice trailed off. He tore the tiny cross from his neck and hurled it across the rubble. From his pocket he took another amulet, a pentacle fashioned from silver, his only possession of any material worth.

I could sell this… it occurred to him. My schoolroom could have its new roof and there would be enough for cakes for the boys come Lammastide…

The metal star grew hot in his hand and seemed to sting him like a wasp.

No.

A murky thought surfaced from the deepest recesses of his mind. This star has other uses…

He held it to the sky so that it framed the sun. Then he inverted the amulet. One point down, two points up…

"Very well," the former prior resolved. "I shall serve you instead, my Lord."

***

Stevens was on the edge of his seat. Alfred Abbott, gratified by the effect he had had on his audience, took a sip from a cup of tea, tepid now from neglect.

"So," Stevens spoke animatedly, "the old prior turned to the dark side and – and – what? Bet he gave that stuck-up headmaster what fucking for."

Alfred Abbott smirked. "Not exactly, but I believe that what happened next will be more directly pertinent to your investigation…"

13.

Stuck in traffic in Miller's car, Brough leafed through *The History of the Occult in the Black Country*, reading out the juiciest titbits, while Miller tried her best not to swear at the slowcoach driver ahead of them or the impatient wanker behind.

"It says here, Miller, that in the 1970s, Dedley was a bit of a magnet for Hell's Angels."

Miller huffed. "What have a load of bearded bikers got to do with the whatsit – the Occult?"

"Our Donald Phillips doesn't say. I think he's clutching at straws to fill a few pages." He flicked through to a different chapter. "Apparently, if you go out on the twenty-eighth of March, you're in very real danger of running into the hell hounds of Halesowen."

"Ooh," said Miller. "I like dogs. Just because he puts 'hell' in front of something, doesn't make it satanic."

"Spot on, Miller. But there's an interesting section here concerning our old mucker Baphomet."

"No friend of mine."

"Quite. It seems there was a spate of grisly deaths in the mid-sixteenth century. A few local merchants, aldermen of the town, people like that. And," he shifted in his seat, "get this, Miller: one was garrotted, one was immolated, one was hanged and another was—"

Angry honking blared from behind.

"The light's green, Miller; you're allowed to proceed."

Miller grunted and drove on. "And when did you pass your test?"

"Never mind that, Miller."

"Man of your age! Can't even drive!"

Brough turned traffic-light red. What was worse than being reminded of his lack of a driving licence was Miller bringing up the 'a' word. And he didn't mean 'arseholes'.

"Eyes on the road, Miller!"

"Are there?" she smiled sourly. "I didn't see them."

They trundled along in disgruntled silence. Miller navigated the one-way system into the town centre.

"Keep your eyes peeled for a parking spot," she instructed him. The closure of Dedley Police station had led to a rapid, almost indecent, selling-off of its car park. An annex of Dedley Technical College was already on the site.

Brough had to get out of the car to guide Miller to a tight space outside the *Nail U Good* manicure parlour.

"And the other?" she asked, locking the car and hitching the strap of her bag onto her shoulder.

"The other what?"

"You said one was garrotted, one was immersed—"

"Immolated!"

"Yes; another was hung—"

"Hanged!"

"And another was – what? The lights went green."

"Ah, yes." He read from the book as they walked to the station. "Another man – a trader, although in what it doesn't say – was torn to pieces."

"Ugh," said Miller. "Does it say how?"

Brough turned a page and read again. "The account is lacking in detail."

"Pity," said Miller. "Might have helped us work out where the next one is going to be."

Brough looked up from the book. "Go on, Miller."

"Well, it seems to me somebody's following the killings in the book. Perhaps it's Donald Phillips himself. Perhaps it's whosit – his son."

"Callum."

"Callum."

"Bloody hell, Miller. You might be on to something. Wait till I tell Wheeler."

He strode ahead.

"Er – sir!" Miller called after him. "Watch out for the—"

Brough skidded and had to cling to a lamppost. He saw what he had trodden in and swore.

Miller grinned. "The hell hounds am out early this year."

***

"Bloody hell, lads; you don't have to follow me in here and all. I don't need nobody to shake it for me."

Si Wren and Bobby Hobley looked uneasily at each other. Their brief, given to them in unequivocal terms, was to stick to the supermarket boss 'like shit to a blanket' – although the longer they spent in the company of Dennis Lord, the poor PCSOs wondered whether they were the blanket.

"Nothing's going to hurt me in there, is it?" Lord jerked his thumb at the door to the male staff toilets. "Perhaps one of you would care to pop in and give it a courtesy flush or warm the fucking seat for me."

"Um, no, you're all right," Si Wren looked at his boots.

"Take your time," suggested Bobby Hobley with a nervous laugh.

"Time's money, bugger-lugs," Dennis Lord patted the PCSO's cheek a little too roughly. "Back in the day, I'd hold it all in, wait until I got home, but nowadays," he pulled out his smartphone, "Thanks to these little babbies, I can conduct business with anybody in the world while I'm on the bastard shitter. Ain't technology bostin'?"

He pushed his way backwards through the door. A few seconds later, Hobley and Wren heard the slam of a cubicle door, followed by a thud as the bolt was rammed home.

The PCSOs backed from the door, dreading the sounds that might follow. Hobley fished out the earbuds attached to his mp3 player and offered one to his colleague.

"Ta," said Wren. "Bit of a twat, isn't he?" He nodded at the door and the horrors beyond.

"The way he talks to people, it's not on. Bastard this and fucking that."

"Remind you of anybody?"

"Ah, well, you see, when she says it, it's different. She's coming from a different place."

"She's not a Dedley wench, then?"

"Oh, ar! Her's from round here all right. What I mean it, when her swears at you, it's because she wants the job done right. That prick in there calls you a shit because he thinks you am one."

Si Wren nodded. He moved his head in time to the tinny track hissing in his earhole. "Love this."

"Tune!" agreed Bobby, swaying in synchronisation with his partner.

***

The phone buzzed insistently, as though an angry bee was trapped inside it. Logger watched it shake and vibrate on the table, too afraid to answer. After what seemed an age, the phone lay still. Logger, realising he had been holding his breath, exhaled.

A beep startled him: a voicemail message.

Logger froze. He had taken the unilateral decision to have nothing more to do with his mystery caller. People he had been asked to target were turning up dead – horribly dead. Murder had not been part of the original bargain.

As though seizing a handful of nettles, Logger picked up the handset and played back the message.

"I don't know what you're playing at, you little shit, but you answer the phone when I call you. We can't afford to let up now.

We must keep applying pressure. Two people are left. I want you to get to them both. I don't care what order you do it. Just don't let me down. There'll be money in the usual place. And erase this fucking message!"

The phone fell silent. Options flashed on the screen:

REPLAY, KEEP, DELETE.

Logger's thumb hovered for a few seconds before he made his choice.

***

"Honestly, Detective Henry, I shall be quite all right from here."

Harry Henry dithered on Beatrice Mooney's doorstep, wondering whether he should point out the latest victim had been hanged in her own home from her own light fitting.

"All right," she relented. "You may come in and check under the bed and in the airing cupboard or anywhere else you see fit, if it will put your mind at ease."

"Cheers." Harry pushed his glasses up his nose and stepped over the threshold. "Won't take long. And we'll have a car outside."

"Well, I should hope it would bloody well be outside," Beatrice Mooney kicked off her shoes and padded along the hall to the kitchen.

"Hold up!" Harry Henry skirted in front of her. He gave the door a cautious push before springing into the kitchen with his eyes darting in all directions. Behind him, Beatrice Mooney laughed; he really was the most ridiculous man.

Her phone rang. The ridiculous detective froze. Rolling her eyes, she answered, moving out of the kitchen and into the hall.

"Yes... yes... Understood," she said, keeping her voice low. "Why must I be the one saddled with...?"

She returned to the kitchen to find Harry Henry with his head in the oven. "Oh, dear! Not that bad is it?"

Harry Henry straightened, banging his head. Beatrice Mooney struggled to contain her laughter.

"I'll just – quickly…" he pointed at the ceiling. He hurried out, rubbing his head.

Ridiculous.

Beatrice Mooney's amusement faded when she realised she was still holding her phone. The call exacerbated her impatience with her so-called police protection. Beatrice Mooney had an itch and she was eager to scratch it – as soon as that ridiculous man was off the premises. She heard him banging about, checking wardrobe doors, the bathroom cabinet… There was a rattle and swish as he pulled aside the shower curtain, bringing it down on top of himself. There was a clunk as the detective toppled into the bath.

I'd be safer without him, Beatrice Mooney reckoned.

And free to do what I want to do.

***

Brough and Miller reported to Dedley nick and showed Chief Inspector Wheeler the book.

"Haven't got time for Jack-a-fucking-nory," she sneered. "Give me the highlights."

While Miller nodded along in support, Brough explained how there had been a slew of murders centuries ago, when merchants and aldermen of the town were slain in ways similar to the crop currently under investigation. The five-pointed star had been drawn at every scene – as described in the book by Donald Phillips, husband of the female victim and father to Callum, one of the hooded vandals from the supermarket.

Wheeler listened. She pulled a face. "And where is this Donald Phillips now?"

Brough and Miller shared a helpless look.

"We have been unable to trace him," said Brough.

"Well, you'd better fucking trace him before we have to trace a chalk line around another fucking victim." She paused; the laugh she expected was not forthcoming.

"Er…" said Miller. "The book says the next one was torn apart."

"That's right," said Brough.

"Does it say how?"

"No…"

Wheeler scratched at her crewcut. "Well, as long as the other two am safe in police protection—" she paled. "What the fuck am I saying? Tell Pattimore and Shit-for-brains to get their arses to Beatrice Mooney's gaff and give our friend Harry a hand. I'm off to the supermarket. Dennis Lord may be the biggest cunt in Dedley but I'd rather he wasn't torn to pieces on my watch."

She dashed from the room just as Pattimore and Shit-for-brains came in.

"What's up with her?" Stevens laughed. "Got the shits, has she?"

"Figuratively, perhaps," said Brough.

"You what?"

"We've been interviewing the deputy head," Pattimore smiled at Brough and nodded at Miller. "He knows a lot of background."

"But you don't think he's responsible," Brough found himself smiling back.

"No."

"Cracking story, though," Stevens enthused. "Lots of horror. Murders, the lot. All it lacked was a woman with big—"

"Here," Brough held out the book to Pattimore. "This tells the same story. See if you can track down the author. Local man."

"Name of Phillips…" Pattimore read the cover. He took the book; his fingers brushed Brough's fingers. Their eyes met.

"As in Callum… um, Phillips," said Brough, unwilling to break eye contact.

"Right!" Stevens snatched the book away and flicked through it. "What's this shit? No fucking pictures?"

"And we'd best be off to look for Callum," suggested Miller, edging to the exit.

"See you later," said Pattimore.

"Um, yes," said Brough, stumbling away. "Oh, yes: Wheeler wants you two to help Harry."

"Right," said Pattimore, with a nod.

Brough nodded back and went out.

Miller waited until they reached her car. "What the hell was that?"

"What the hell was what?"

"You and Jason. The long, lingering looks."

Brough turned red. "I don't know what you're talking about," he lied.

***

"All right, Log?" Dogger zipped up his hoodie and joined his friend at the kerb outside his house. "What's going on?"

"Where's Bonk?"

Dogger laughed. "I'm not his keeper."

"He could do with a keeper," grumbled Logger. He thrust his hands into his hoodie pockets and moved off. Dogger followed suit.

"He's with his brother, I think."

"Shit!" Logger spat.

"At Costbosters."

"Shit!"

"Is something wrong, Log? Have you heard from – you know?"

Logger grunted. "There's two left. He doesn't care what order we do them in – he's leaving that to my wossname."

"You've got a plan! You have! I can see it in your scowl."

Oh, I've got a plan all right, thought Logger darkly. I've got one hell of a plan.

"So, who am they then?"

"Who am who?"

"The two left."

"You'll find out," said Logger, enigmatically. His air of mystery excited Dogger, who skipped alongside him like an eager puppy.

"Right," Logger stopped at the corner. "You fuck off to Costbosters, fetch Bonk. Meet me back here in an hour."

Dogger was a little perturbed by the prospect of splitting up but he nodded obediently. "Um, what about Callum?"

"What about him?"

"Shall I fetch him and all?"

Logger shook his head emphatically. "Let's leave that specky twat out of this one, shall we?"

"Oh," Dogger looked surprised. "More money for us, I suppose."

"Go on, then; off you toddle. Fetch Bonk like a good boy."

Dogger saluted but he stayed where he was. "Where am you going?"

"Never you mind!" Logger snapped, startling him. "Never you fucking mind."

***

Callum negotiated his way over the stile, using the carrier bags of food as ballast. Visions of tightrope-walking sprang to mind; I could still run away to the circus, he mused sourly.

He jumped to the gravel path, his eyes darting around. There were no cars on the square patch of paved area and the visitor centre wouldn't be open for another month at least. Dedley's nature reserve was world-renowned – well, among those who held such things in esteem – for its limestone caverns and its abundance of fossils – but it was not open to the public all year round. Thus, for now, it made the perfect meeting place.

Bring offerings, the Goat Man had said. Bring sacrificial offerings.

Callum had spent his allowance on a wide range of foodstuffs – from *Cigs, Figs and Wigs*. He'd deemed it prudent to keep away

126

from *CostBusters* for a while. He hadn't known what to bring exactly so he'd bought something to represent each of the five major food groups. The Goat Man had been less than specific but, now that he thought about it, Callum supposed meat would be the preferred option.

Well, it's a good job I bought those southern-fried chicken portions then, isn't it?

He skirted the visitor centre, taking time to admire the view. The Squirrel's Hole nature reserve was at the top of a range of hills, exceeded in height only by the mound that was home to Dedley Castle and its zoological gardens a mile away. At the foot of these hills nestled a council estate that shared the nature reserve's name as though that would render it more picturesque and appealing.

What an eyesore, Callum thought! At least one of the trio of idiots lived down there in that squalor. Perhaps all three did; Callum did not care to know.

The path became less maintained and more irregular and took him away from the cabin where visitors could pick up leaflets and cups of tea and through denser undergrowth. Callum had to take more care where he stepped. A thorny tendril snatched at one of his carrier bags, tearing a hole when Callum pulled it away.

"Oh, no, you don't!" he snapped, and immediately felt foolish. Shouting at a shrub! I'm nervous, he supposed.

The path curved and sloped downward, taking him away from the view of the estate. Loose stones rolled from his footsteps like skittish mice. Dropping steeply, the path took him to the mouth of one of the caverns. Despite outcry from many naturalists and palaeontologists, the entrance had been filled with concrete 'for reasons of health and safety'. The once-smooth surface was now pockmarked and covered with graffiti; the place was still a favourite haunt of locals. A smattering of used condoms and discarded syringes was testament to this fact.

Callum waited; it was the designated spot. Here, the old prior had been run to ground and sealed in a cave, all because he had executed his rivals and tormentors. It hardly seemed fair. Callum had read it in the book that had appeared, as if by magic, on the desk in his bedroom one day.

Time was ticking by. Mum would be wondering what had happened to him, he reckoned. *Perhaps I should give her a call…*

There was no signal. *Oh, well.*

The late afternoon sun was low, shining almost directly into his eyes. His spectacles glinted in the glare. He squinted until a merciful cloud rolled across the offending orb. A shadowy figure was revealed, standing on a nearby outcrop, towering over the scene.

Callum gasped. The figure was sporting a long, tattered coat that reached the ground, a cowl that cast his face in shadow and – Callum hoped it was a headpiece – a pair of curling horns.

Behold! The Goat Man!

"There you are, my boy!" the horned figure spread his arms in a welcoming gesture.

The cloud moved on its way and Callum was dazzled again.

***

"Excuse me," said Brough to the man who was trying to enter Dedley nick as he and Miller were trying to get out of it.

"Sorry," said the man, and then, "Excuse me."

Brough nodded and kept walking.

"No, I mean excuse me as in 'please may I have your attention for a moment?'"

Brough stopped and turned. Miller was in the doorway, looking the man up and down and smiling.

"Yes?" Brough's tone was gruff.

"Do you work here?"

"Yes!" said Miller. The man ignored her.

"We don't deal with parking tickets," Brough warned impatiently.

"We'm detectives," added Miller. This caught the man's attention.

"Good," he said. "Then perhaps you can tell me what the fuck's going on at my house."

"I'm sorry?" said Brough.

"I arrive home to find it all taped off and a constable at the gate who won't breathe a word."

"Ah," said Miller.

"Oh," said Brough, only now registering the man's agitated state. Distress had formed a sheen of sweat on his brow.

"You must be Donald Phillips," said Miller.

"I think we'd all better go inside," said Brough.

14.

"I can hear you muttering," Charlie West admonished his brother. "It won't do you no good, muttering. And put that tabard on, like I told you."

Bonk's lip curled, a dog ready to snarl, but even he knew better than to yip and snap at the hand that fed him. He shrugged on the luminescent yellow waistcoat, catching his hood at the back. Charlie rolled his eyes.

"Come here." He extricated the hood from its confines. "Although I don't know why you have to wear the bloody thing. Gives people the wrong idea. You're not a bad lad, Nat. Deep down. You've just got in with a bad crowd, that's all."

Bonk squirmed out of Charlie's clutches. "Nothing wrong with my friends," he scowled. "Least I've got some."

This remark earned him a flick to the ear but it was Charlie who was stung the deeper.

"Well, maybe if I wasn't working every bloody shift I can to keep you in Monster Munch and hooded jackets, I'd be able to get out there and live a little. You selfish prick. Now, come on."

"Do I have to?"

"We've been through this. Yes, you have to. You're going to stack shelves until you've paid off the damage you and your nothing-wrong-with-them friends caused the other day."

"Not fair," Bonk muttered.

But he followed his brother out to the shop floor, prepared to do as he was told.

***

Chief Inspector Karen Wheeler slammed the car door. She locked it with a click of her key ring while her other hand tried to call Dennis bastard Lord yet again. She saw there was no signal and swore.

Probably because I'm in the car park, she reasoned, holding her phone at arm's length – which wasn't very far at all. Overhead loomed the underbelly of the supermarket. It's like the world's most fucking boring cave, she sneered in disdain. She strode through the plate glass doors, which had sense (or sensors) enough to part company and get out of her way. The mood I'm in, they wouldn't have stopped me, she huffed.

She swerved past the traditional staircase and rode the stairless elevator to the shop floor, all the while waving her phone around, like a child with a sparkler on Bonfire Night. Three little bars appeared at the top of the screen. Signal at last but still no bastard answer.

And, of course, Chimp One and Chimp Two were not at their post. The trestle table was deserted, its sign hanging askew. Neither were they in the *Queequeg's* – No, of course not, Karen, you dozy twat – they'll be wherever that wankstain is.

Or they'd better bloody bastard bloody be.

Fuming, she revolved on the spot, tapping her foot. Lord would have an office or something, a fucking rock to crawl under, somewhere behind the scenes. Where might that be?

She cast around, looking for inspiration. Her gaze fell on that pleasant young man, the security guard she had encountered on her previous visit. *He* would know.

"Hello, Fuck-knuckle!" she greeted him with a smile as she approached.

"Er…" Charlie West was a little thrown. "Um, hello, Chief Inspector. How lovely to see—"

"Don't you fucking lie to my fucking face," she cut him off. "I'm a pain in the scrotum. But if you tell me what I want to know, I'll evaporate like the fucking morning dew."

"Right," grinned Charlie West. "How the fuck may I be of assistance?"

Wheeler grinned back. "I like you, Charlie. Take me to your leader."

***

Brough and Miller waited while the news sank in. Donald Phillips's face worked as he processed the knowledge that his wife was dead – murdered in their own home – and their son was – what was he? Missing? A suspect?

Miller pushed a box of tissues across the table. Donald Phillips stared at it, not understanding.

"We appreciate," said Brough, "that this is hitting you hard but, Mr Phillips, anything you can tell us – anything at all – could prove vital to our investigation."

Donald Phillips shook his head and frowned. "I don't know anything – I can't think – I…"

Miller sent Brough a hard look but he persisted.

"Perhaps you can tell us about this." He pushed something across the table. Donald Phillips glanced up – it wasn't a box of tissues. It was a book.

"What? What do you mean?"

"You've seen this before."

"Not for years. Why? Where did you get it?"

"We found it in your house, Mr Phillips. In your son's room."

Donald Phillips looked like he had been kicked in the face. "Damn. Damn it! I thought I'd got rid of that."

"You didn't want your son to read it?"

"I don't want anyone to read it. Load of codswallop. Some might say dangerous codswallop."

"You regret it, then?"

"Regret what?" A penny dropped. Donald Phillips snatched up *A History of the Occult in the Black Country* and pointed at the name on the cover. "That's not me! I didn't write it."

"You didn't write this book?" said Brough.

"I'm a salesman. I sell ball bearings. I can barely write a text message."

"You're not Donald Phillips?" said Miller.

"I am! But not that Donald Phillips. That Donald Phillips is my father."

***

Bonk lost himself in his work. This was something he could cope with, something he could do. He reached another jar of peanut butter from the trolley and placed it on the shelf, turning it so that its label faced front, taking his time to get it exactly right. He stepped back to evaluate his work and stepped on Dogger's foot.

"Ow!" Dogger gave Bonk a punch and shoved him away. "Watch where you'm going."

"Hello, Dog," said Bonk. "Can't talk now. Got shelves to load."

"Fuck me," said Dogger. "What's happened to you?"

"Not now," said Bonk. "Leave me alone."

He picked up another jar.

"Logger says to meet him. We've got two to do tonight."

"I'm not coming," said Bonk, unable to meet Dogger's eye. "Got work to do."

"Bonk!" Dogger stepped closer, his voice more urgent. "Have they done something to you?"

"Gerroff!" Bonk backed away. "Don't make me call security."

"Your brother? You're going to set your big brother on me? Bonk, it's me, Dogger!" He waved his hand in front of Bonk's eyes. "Snap out of it!"

"I'm serious, Dog," Bonk stuck his nose in the air. "Go; play your childish pranks. I'm a grown-up now."

Dogger laughed. "Logger's not going to believe this."

"I don't give a monkey's," sniffed Bonk. He turned his back and resumed his task.

Dogger stared at him, incredulous. He looked at the time. Logger would be waiting. He gave the trolley a kick and stormed off, leaving Bonk to concentrate on aligning his jars with his tongue jutting from the corner of his mouth.

***

All the offices were empty – the staff who worked in them tended to go home at five, Charlie West explained. Wheeler didn't seem interested. "Just find me the bastard," she grunted.

"There is one place we haven't tried," Charlie was suddenly inspired. "This way."

They strode through the staff canteen – an ostrich being followed by a penguin – and to a corridor labelled with pictures of a man and a woman.

"Ta-dah!" said Charlie, extending his arm to show the two PCSOs slumped against the wall, connected by earbuds and, apparently, asleep.

Wheeler kicked the sole of Hobley's shoe. The PCSO stirred. His eyelids flickered and then sprang apart.

"Wakey, wakey, sweetheart," Wheeler cooed. Somehow this was more terrifying than a barrage of expletives. Galvanised, Hobley jumped up. The other earbud was yanked from Wren's ear with a resounding pop – Wren sank to the floor. The impact woke him up.

When both PCSOs were standing to something like attention, Wheeler looked them each in the eye and then showed them her teeth. She forced words out between them.

"Where – the – fuck – is – he?"

Wren and Hobley seemed to relax a little, relieved it was an easy question.

"In there," Wren jerked his thumb at the door to the Gents.

"Having a shit," Hobley added, pleased to be helpful.

"And how long," Wheeler's chest rose, "has he been in there?"

Hobley and Wren looked at each other and pulled faces. Wren checked his watch; his jaw dropped.

"Quite a bit, actually," he squeaked. Wheeler's stare bore into him. "Three hours!" he cringed.

"Three fucking hours!" Wheeler exploded. "Well, I know that fucker is full of fucking shit but three fucking hours is taking the fucking piss, don't you think?"

She nodded to Charlie, who nodded back and pushed open the door. He went in; Wheeler followed but the hobby-bobbies hung back in the doorway, fearful for their lives.

Even the most cursory inspection revealed that the bogs were empty, 'completely devoid of bastards' as Wheeler put it.

"Perhaps the fucking fucker flushed himself," she mused, peering into a toilet bowl. "No, he's too big of a shit to get around the S bend."

She turned her attention to the ceiling. People were always escaping through the ceiling on the telly. They made it look so easy. You just climb up, dislodge a tile and crawl away to freedom.

"Over here," said Charlie West. He was standing by the window – the open window that gave out on to a fire escape.

Wheeler peered over the windowsill. Dennis Lord was long gone.

"Fucking shit," she snarled.

Behind her, the PCSOs whimpered.

***

D I Stevens rapped a tattoo on the bonnet of D I Henry's car, startling the poor man in the driving seat out of his catnap.

"Harry!" Stevens grinned. "Asleep on the job, are we? You'll cop it when Wheeler finds out."

"Ignore him," said Pattimore, opening the door. Harry climbed out.

"I generally do," he said, pushing his spectacles back up his nose.

"We've come to help," said Pattimore, looking at Beatrice Mooney's house. "Behaving herself, is she?"

"Good as gold," said Harry. "Haven't heard a peep."

"You have been checking on her, Haz?" Stevens brows dipped in a frown. "Every half hour."

"Well – um – Don't call me 'Haz'!" Harry Henry looked both hurt and defensive.

"Jesus Christ," Stevens wailed. He jogged up the path to the front door. Pattimore and Henry followed.

The house was in darkness. No lights, not even the television.

"Um, perhaps she's gone to bed," Harry Henry offered.

"At six o'fucking clock?" Stevens was scornful. "To quote one of my favourite film stars, I'm going in the back door."

He moved around the side of the house. Pattimore gave Harry Henry a baleful look.

"Oh, Harry," he said.

"Oh, crumbs," said Harry Henry.

15.

How romantic! Beatrice Mooney giggled to herself. All this sneaking around in the dark! A secret rendezvous!

All right, so climbing over the fence in her own back garden hadn't been her most elegant moment, and stumbling through the undergrowth to make her way to the road had almost caused her to twist an ankle. But it would be worth it.

It better be worth it.

What am I going to do, give him lines, put him in detention? She laughed at herself. It was a bit of fun, that's all. A bit of slap and tickle in the stables.

All the same, now that I've eluded the police, he'd better bloody show up.

She stole across the stable yard, barely able to contain her excited laughter. She kept a horse there but didn't get to ride him as often as she liked. Poor Dazzler!

I'm here for a ride of a different kind! She laughed and tiptoed into the stable to get herself ready.

***

"And you've no idea where we might contact your father," Brough rubbed his eyes.

"Like I said, he's homeless," said Donald Phillips Junior. "We haven't heard from him in a long time."

"Your own father!" said Miller. Phillips caught the accusation in her tone.

"Listen," he looked the female detective in the eye. "It's not what you think. He's ill. Very ill. He was in a home – for people with mental problems. But he got away. Lived rough for a while

137

and then when they took him back, the home had closed down. Fucking austerity, they call it. Oh, we can't have him with us – he's too much of a liability – I mean, we can't give him the care he needs. I say 'we' but…"

His voice trailed off. He had just reminded himself that his wife was dead.

"Mr Phillips," said Brough, not ungently, "What kind of illness are we talking about here?"

"I told you," Donald Phillips sniffed. "Mental illness. I don't know the technical term. Paranoid schizophrenia – something like that. Perhaps it was messing about with all that devil bullshit that screwed him up. Research for his book. It sort of took him over – and no, I don't mean demonic possession. I don't believe in it. But then there was the accident. Got himself kicked in the head. By a goat, of all things. Had to have a metal plate fitted. He hasn't been right since."

Brough and Miller shared a glance. Donald Phillips caught that too.

"You think he's doing this?" He gestured at the book on the table, as though it was his father's representative.

"It's a possibility we're considering," said Brough.

Donald Phillips shook his head. "I can't believe it. He wouldn't—" He stopped himself. "My God! Callum! Do you think he's got Callum?"

"We don't know," said Miller.

"Your son's whereabouts are still unknown," said Brough.

Donald Phillips put his face in his hands. "Find him!" he urged the detectives.

"Who?" said Miller. "Your dad? Or your son?"

"Both," said Donald Phillips. "Please!"

***

Callum watched the Goat Man build a small fire and skewer a piece of southern fried chicken on a twig and hold it over the flames. To the boy's inexpert eye, it looked less like a sacrificial offering and more like a spot of campfire cuisine.

"Still here, boy?" the Goat Man looked up from his cooking. "You're a good lad—" he paused, cocking his head to one side. He appeared to be listening to something, something Callum couldn't hear.

The Goat Man nodded his hooded head, as though agreeing with something.

"Tell me, my boy," his eyes twinkled beneath their shadowy covering, "Is there a stable around here?"

"Um," Callum thought about it. "I think so. Couple of miles. Why? Do you need a horse?"

The thought amused him. A goat riding a horse!

"Not the horse, no…" the Goat Man chuckled enigmatically. He dropped the chicken into the fire and then kicked dirt over it, extinguishing the flames and burying the portion. Callum expected him to say something, an incantation in Latin or something, but all the Goat Man did was wipe his fingers on his already greasy coat and head off.

"Come on, boy!" he called over his shoulder. "Don't dawdle!"

Callum stumbled after him. The Goat Man was more surefooted in his strides along the path. Well, he would be, thought Callum. He's probably got cloven hooves inside those boots.

The Goat Man stood proudly on the stile, turning his head in all directions. The curls of his horns glinted in the street light. "Which way, boy? To the stable?"

"Down the hill and up toward Gornal," said Callum. "Follow me!"

Now, there's a spot of role reversal, he thought!

***

Detectives Pattimore, Stevens and Henry gathered in Beatrice Mooney's kitchen. They turned on the spot, at a loss.

"She ain't here," said Stevens, in case the others hadn't worked that out for themselves.

"She's vanished!" said Harry Henry. "It's all my fault!"

"No, it's not," said Pattimore. "You can't be expected to watch both sides of a house at the same time on your own. We should have got here sooner."

Harry Henry gasped, "It's all your fault!"

"Fuck off," said Stevens.

"We're not here to apportion blame," said Pattimore. "Let's try and work out where she might have gone."

"She could have buggered off anywhere," said Stevens.

Harry Henry pointed. "There's a calendar on the wall."

Beneath a glossy photograph of a horse, a grid laid out the days of the month. The detectives peered at it. Various appointments were scrawled on it. Meetings were circled. But there was nothing to indicate where Beatrice Mooney might have buggered off to that evening.

"This is bollocks," Stevens groaned, "Like looking for a clitoris in a haystack."

"I think I've put my finger on it," said Pattimore.

"First time for everything," said Stevens.

Pattimore took a leaflet from the fridge door. It had been held in place by a horseshoe-shaped magnet. "Bit horsey, our headmistress."

"I don't know," said Stevens. "She was all right."

"Not looks," said Pattimore. "Interests." He riffled through the other papers displayed on the fridge. "Invoices, vets' bills…"

"You think she rode off into the fucking sunset?"

"It's a possibility," said Pattimore. "Unless you've got a better idea?"

"Um," Harry Henry was already thumbing his smartphone. "Stable's not far from here. Up near Gornal."

"Feels like we'm clutching at straws," said Stevens.

"What else have we got?" said Pattimore.

Harry Henry waved a finger. "She did have a phone call. While I was here, checking the house."

"Who from?" said Stevens.

"I don't know," Harry admitted. "Something private, I know that."

"Think, Harry! Did she say anything that might indicate..."

"Um..." Harry Henry's forehead furrowed. He took off his glasses and wiped them on his knitted tie.

"This is a waste of fucking time," said Stevens.

"Um," said Harry Henry. "Come to think of it, she did mention something about being *saddled* with something."

"Good enough!" said Pattimore. "Come on!"

* * *

Brough and Miller delivered Donald Phillips to the Railway Hotel – he couldn't go home just yet and neither did he wish to. In the car, heading back to the nick, Brough pored over the book, searching for ideas.

"Torn apart... torn apart..." he flicked back and forth. "If you were going to tear someone apart, Miller, how would you do it?"

"With my bare hands!" Miller laughed. "If I was angry enough."

"I don't doubt it for a second. But how would a mere mortal go about it, do you think?"

"I don't know. I remember an old film, set in a jungle or somewhere. They got this bloke and they tied him to these trees. They'd pulled the treetops down and tied them to the ground, tied the bloke between them, cut the ropes or whatever and whoosh, he goes flying through the air in different directions all at once."

"Ugh," said Brough. "It's a possibility, I suppose. Where in Dedley are there trees?"

"Oh, there's one or two dotted around," said Miller. "Field Park, for example."

Brough nodded. "You're making sense, Miller."

"First time for everything!"

"No, no; I'm sure it's happened before."

His phone rang. Pattimore.

"Jason! Hi! How are – things? At Mooney's house, I mean." Brough cleared his throat; Miller rolled her eyes. Brough listened. "No!... And what makes you think she's gone there?... Makes sense, I suppose... Do you want me on your back? I mean, to back you up? I mean, do you want back-up? Not necessarily me, but... Well, keep in touch, yeah?"

He put his phone away just as Miller pulled on the handbrake.

"Everything OK?" she asked, pointedly.

"She's run off. Beatrice Mooney. You know, the head teacher. Jas – *Pattimore* reckons she's gone to the stable where she keeps a horse."

"Does he now?"

"Yes. It's as good a place to start as any."

"I'm not disagreeing," Miller laughed, "You don't have to be so defensive on his behalf."

"I'm not being."

"Think about it. Horses. They could tear somebody apart no trouble."

"Not more old films, Miller?"

"Yes, as a matter of fact. Used to watch them with my mom. Only thing that held her attention at the end, in that home. They reminded her of the old days."

"When she used to tear people apart with horses?"

"No, silly. When we used to watch old films together when I was a girl."

Brough nodded. "It's not a completely implausible scenario, I suppose. Well done, Miller."

"Can I have that in writing?"

Brough's phone rang a second time. Wheeler.

He had to hold the handset away from his ear; there was never a need to put the chief inspector on loudspeaker.

They listened to her diatribe. Between the swearwords and the railing against the police community support officers – in general and in particular – they gathered that supermarket magnate Dennis Lord had gone AWOL, and Wheeler didn't have a fucking clue where.

When he could get a word in, Brough brought her up to speed with Pattimore's news. This gave rise to more swearing but that was no surprise.

"Shall we go to the stables as well, Chief?" Brough sounded hopeful; Miller noticed.

"Nah," said Wheeler. "Get your arses to the supermarket. By the time you get here, I might have thought of something to do with you."

Brough pocketed his phone and caught Miller's eye. "What are you smirking at, Miller?"

Miller grinned. "Nothing. Sir."

***

"Where is he?"

"Where's who?" said Dogger.

"Bonk, you twat," Logger was annoyed. Dogger explained about Bonk's weird behaviour in the supermarket. Logger was philosophical. "Oh, well. We can do without him. Come on."

Dogger had to hurry to keep up. "Where am we going?"

"Just hurry up," said Logger, without looking back. "The stables near Gornal – do you know them?"

Dogger pulled a face. "Should I?" Then he brightened. "Am we getting a horse, then? Log! Log! Am we getting a horse?"

"Not exactly," said Logger. "I had a message. That's where the next target will be."

"What then?"

"You'll see when we get there," said Logger.

Hoods up and hands in pockets, the two boys skulked through the streets, leaving Dedley behind. Ahead, the village of Gornal nestled around the base of a hill. Beyond it, the green belt and the stables.

A popular destination, all of a sudden.

16.

Dogger tugged at Logger's sleeve. "There's a light on," he whispered. "Somebody's here!"

Logger shook him off. It was true: the dim glow of lamplight shone weakly from the stable. "Be a pussy all your life," he sneered. "It's probably just a night light for the 'osses."

Dogger blinked. "Really? Really, Log? Is that what they do?"

"I don't bloody know, do I?"

In his annoyance with Dogger, Logger momentarily forgot he was supposed to be sneaking around. A few yards from the building he slowed his stride to a creep and hunched his shoulders. Dogger did the same; he didn't like being in Logger's bad books – with Bonk otherwise engaged, Dogger was the only one in the firing line.

They snuck toward the stable door, which was closed but not bolted, and flattened themselves against the wall like they had seen on the telly. Logger took something out of his hoodie, something cylindrical and black. Dogger's eyes widened.

"You'm going to hit her!" he breathed, both astonished and appalled. "You'm going to cosh old Mooney!"

Logger frowned. "No!" He unrolled the cylinder. "It's bin bags, you fanny."

"You'm going to put her in a bin bag."

"Not exactly. Now, shut your gob and follow me."

He dropped into a crouch and gave the door a gentle push.

Inside, in a stall, Beatrice Mooney was on tenterhooks. She was also beginning to get cramp in her knees. Hardly a patient woman in the best of circumstances, she was two minutes away from giving up on the whole palaver and going back home.

The horses in the neighbouring stalls stirred, hoofing the floor and snorting. Beatrice Mooney tensed. At bloody last, he was here!

She attempted to dispel her irritation and get herself into a mood more appropriate for the activity ahead. She listened – she could barely hear the shuffling of feet amid the growing disquiet of the stable's equine residents. It sounded like he was going from stall to stall, when she had distinctly told him which one she would be in. Why do people never listen?

And there was the irritation again! Perhaps he was deliberately trying to piss her off, she wondered. Perhaps it was another of his kinks.

A pair of feet appeared under her stall door. Scruffy Converse that had seen better days. Odd, thought Beatrice Mooney, holding her breath. She had been expecting green wellies.

And then a second pair of similarly scruffy footwear appeared. She certainly had not been expecting that. Perhaps it was going to be kinkier than she had imagined. Two rugged stable hands to break in the bucking bronco...

"Ready?" said a voice.

"Ready?" answered the other.

Before Beatrice Mooney could think, two pairs of hands were raised over the stall door, shaking bin bags of freshly gathered horse manure all over the cowering head teacher.

Beatrice Mooney screamed and caught a mouthful of dung. Gagging and gasping, she flung open the stall door, startling two hooded boys who staggered backwards in shock. She was unable to stand up straight with a saddle on her back, so she scrambled around on all fours, coughing and shouting, arching her back as though trying to throw an invisible rider.

Logger and Dogger clung to each other as their head teacher reared up and rolled around, her face a vivid shade of purple. In their stalls, the other horses whinnied and screamed and stamped.

"Oh, fuck," said Dogger.

"Let's fuck off," suggested Logger. The youths headed to the exit, each carrying a bulging bin bag. They made their escape just seconds before the headlights of a Ford Capri stretched their beams across the yard.

"Fuck me," Dogger panted. "That was close."

"One down, one to go," said Logger. He thrust his bag at Dogger's chest. "Carry this, will you? I've got a stitch."

***

The Goat Man came to a sudden halt. Callum almost walked right into him. Puzzled, he watched as the Goat Man tilted his head this way and that, angling his horns in different directions.

"Sir?" said Callum, after a minute of this.

The Goat Man sprang around. "Change of plan, my boy!"

He strode off, back the way they had come. Callum hurried after.

"We're not going to the stables, then?"

"Not anymore," the Goat Man called back without turning around.

"Oh." Callum was disappointed. He had envisaged some kind of unholy ritual, a counteraction to that holy night in a stable long ago and far away. The opposite of a birth. "Where are we going now?"

The Goat Man took the road that would lead them to the town centre.

"Up!" said the Goat Man, pointing at the evening sky. "We're going up in the world!"

***

Chief Inspector Wheeler rubbed her eyes with the heels of her hands. It had been a long day and there was something about spending time with a couple of shit-for-brains hobby bobbies that was making the day stretch into a fortnight.

"I know I'm asking the fucking impossible," she groaned, "But think, for fuck's sake! You was with him all bloody day before he morphed into Harry fucking Houdini. Did he say or do anything that might tell us where he pissed off to? Any calls that he received, any calls that he made? Any fucking thing at all!"

Si Wren and Bobby Hobley looked at their laps, certain the shouty lady would commence waterboarding them at any second. They were sitting side by side in the office of their absentee charge while the chief inspector railed at them. There was something of a hostage situation to the scene.

Si Wren let out a squeak. From his anus. Wheeler rounded on him. With him seated and her standing, they were eye to eye. He recoiled from her stark, ophidian stare.

At Wren's side, Bobby Hobley stifled a yelp of terror – it escaped from his nostril in the form of a snot bubble.

Wheeler despaired. "Frig my labia like Lawrence of Arabia."

"Um," said Bobby Hobley with a wet sniff. "We didn't think it polite to earwig."

"It's – manners," added Si Wren.

"Oh, is it?" Wheeler roared. "Well, pardon me, Little Lord Fuck-Knuckle, we wouldn't want you to do anything that might offend your dear mama! Close your eyes! Both of you! Now!"

The PCSOs jumped. Hobley yelped. Wren reached for his hand. They were certain their time was up. There was no saying what the nasty, shouty lady would do to them but they were guessing it might involve bowls of ice-water and electrodes.

"Keep 'em closed!" Wheeler warned. They could hear her walking around them – *prowling* around the chairs. "Keep them fucking peepers fucking well shut! Now, I want you to fucking relax. I want you to relive your time with our mutual friend, Mr Dennis Lord, and I want you to retrace every footstep, rehear every fucking word."

Si Wren fidgeted on his chair. Bobby Hobley's head lolled. He snored.

"Fuck sake," said Chief Inspector Wheeler.

There was a knock at the door; the PCSOs almost jumped out of their hi-viz tabards. Charlie West's head popped into the office.

"What the fuck do you want?" Wheeler snapped.

"Um – not sure if it's of any use but we've just taken delivery of tomorrow's Dedley Chronicle."

"Let me get the fucking flags out."

"No, but this might help." Charlie pushed open the door and held out a copy of the latest edition of the local paper.

His hand's not shaking, Wheeler was pleased to note. Unlike Bubble and Squeak who were quivering like terrified jellies in an earthquake. She read the headline. Her expression brightened.

"Charlie West," she grinned, "I could fucking fuck you red raw."

"Please don't," said Charlie West.

***

Logger and Dogger swaggered into CostBusters as if they owned the place, swinging bulging bin bags at their sides. They strolled along the aisles, looking for the third member of their triumvirate.

"We could ask him," Dogger pointed out a member of staff who was building a pyramid from cans of baked beans. "Hey, mate, you seen a kid called Bonk? I mean Nat West. As in the bonk, do you get it?"

The shelf-stacker turned. "Do you know, I've never got it until now?"

The others gaped. It was Bonk, but his hair was combed, his hands and face were clean and he was standing up straight. Crucially, he was no longer sporting his hooded jacket.

"Christ, Bonk," said Logger, feeling the sting of betrayal.

"What have they done to you?" gasped Dogger. "Have they swapped you with an alien?"

"Soz, lads," said Bonk. "Cor speak to you right now. I'm on the clock."

Dogger and Logger let out cries of horror.

"What happened to you, man?" Dogger was incredulous.

"I doubt it's brain-washing," said Logger. "Listen, Bonk, we'll get out of your way if you tell us where the boss's office is."

Bonk's heavy brows dipped in a frown of suspicion. "Why?"

"We want to see him," said Logger, finding himself adopting a rather business-like tone.

"Got him a present," Dogger held out a bin bag. Logger nudged him to lower it again.

"He ain't there," said Bonk. "They'm all looking for him. The coppers. Everybody. Even my brother."

"Hmm," said Logger. "And you've no idea where he's gone?"

"Who? My Charlie? He went into the office to show the cops the paper."

"What paper?"

"This one." Bonk led them away. "We've got stacks of them."

***

The Serious team reconvened at Dedley nick. Stevens and Pattimore had brought a red-faced Beatrice Mooney in for safe-keeping. She was in an interview room, trying to live down her humiliation and she was keeping her lips buttoned over the identity of her no-show lover. Stevens couldn't stop sniggering.

"It's like this video I downloaded the other night. *Rodeo Bitches*."

Miller cut her eyes at him. "Didn't that win this year's Oscar for best screenplay?"

Stevens shook his head. "Well, it certainly didn't win Best Costume. Because there weren't none!"

Brough raised his voice. "If we could focus on the case?"

"Brough's right," said Pattimore. "There's still a potential victim out there. And a killer too."

150

Brough sent him a grateful smile, which did not go unnoticed by Miller. Christ, she thought.

"With Ms Mooney tucked away—"

"Yee-hah!" Stevens interrupted.

"—it is our best guess that the killer will go after Dennis Lord who, as it turns out, has eluded the PCSOs. And Chief Inspector Wheeler herself."

The team sucked in air, picturing how incandescent with rage their boss would be at that moment. Harry Henry raised a hand.

"Yes, Harry?" Brough nodded.

"Um," he stood – every time for Harry Henry, getting to his feet was reminiscent of a new-born fawn taking its first steps. "We think the killer might try to tear Dennis Lord apart in some way. It probably won't be horses, as we thought with—"

"Bucking Beatrice!" Stevens interjected, slapping his thigh.

"—Ms Mooney," Harry continued. "So we need alternative ideas."

Brough grinned. "Harry… I can tell by the look on your face, you already have an idea."

Harry Henry's cheeks grew hot. He waved his smartphone. "I've been looking into ways they used to kill people back in the day. We've seen a hanging, a garrotting, an immolation—"

"A what?" blinked Stevens.

"Setting on fire," the rest of the team chorused.

"Go on, Harry," Brough encouraged.

"Um, well, according to local history, the next person was torn apart, but I want to look at it another way."

"Put back together, do you mean?" scoffed Stevens.

Everyone ignored him.

"There's this thing they used to do, where they'd tie someone to a wheel and—"

Harry's exposition was interrupted yet again, this time by the telephone. Brough answered. The others heard at once the far-from-dulcet tones of Chief Inspector Wheeler. Brough had to hold the receiver away from his ear in order to prevent damage to his hearing.

The team listened to Wheeler's irate monologue, punctuated with swearwords rather than intakes of breath. At long last, Brough hung up.

"Well," he addressed the others, "you heard the lady. Let's get our 'fucking arses' down to the Dedley Eye. Harry, it looks like there might be something in this wheel idea of yours. Good man!"

Harry Henry gushed. His glasses fell off.

The Serious team filed out. Miller hung back, waiting for Brough.

"Oh, I don't need a lift, Miller; it's only around the block."

"Suit yourself."

At the door, she turned back. "You'm up to something, aren't you, David Brough? I can see your mind working from here."

Brough smirked. "I do have a smidgeon of an idea, yes. And, on second thought, you can give me a lift, Miller, but not to the Eye. There's something I need to collect."

17.

Dennis Lord bunged the night-watchman a handful of fifty-pound notes and instructed him to piss off out of it. The man didn't need to be told twice. The boss was the boss. He handed Mr Lord the keys and skittered away, heading for the off-licence and the takeaway on his way home for an unexpected night off.

Dennis Lord laughed to himself, feeling like a child sneaking downstairs on Christmas Day to open his presents before the rest of the household got up.

Tomorrow would be the unveiling. The Mayor would be there, the local paps – Dennis Lord had his speech all ready already. Never a patient man, he wanted to make sure that the first bum on any of those seats was his. And so, a little test drive was called for. In fact, it made bloody good sense. He needed to familiarise himself with the controls and the machinery so he wouldn't look a complete tit when he started it up in front of the crowd.

The 'it' in question was a gigantic Ferris wheel of slender, white tubular steel, for the moment shrouded from view by tarpaulin sheets. He had had it shipped over from Paris at his own expense – that was what he was telling people but he was secure in the knowledge that his accountants would have more than covered the outgoings with tax loopholes and the like.

My gift to the town that whelped me, he was planning to announce as he cut the ribbon with an overly large pair of scissors. It would attract visitors. And visitors meant income. And a giant supermarket that had leached the lifeblood from the town centre would rake in the extra cash…

Dennis Lord's eyes glinted as he imagined the sound of old-fashioned cash registers ringing in his ears.

He unfastened the padlock on the chain that held the temporary wire-frame fence together. The fence encircled the foot of the wheel and would be gone before the crowds assembled in the square.

It was funny, he reflected, the last time this paved patch of ground had seen any action was four or five years back when it had hosted a beer festival in a tent. That had gone tits-up, he seemed to recall, when somebody had got himself murdered.

He shivered. Perhaps on this very spot...

Nah, couldn't happen again, he told himself.

He slipped through the fence and tugged at a rope. The sheets of tarpaulin slid from the wheel, revealing it in all its glory – he would pay somebody to put it all back again first thing in the morning. When you have enough money, you can get anybody to do anything.

At least he knew the rope worked. It would be a dramatic moment.

He found a flat, square-headed key and inserted it into a control panel on the base of the wheel. He twisted it by ninety degrees and a chunky red light came on. He only had to push that glowing button and the Dedley Eye would begin to turn...

Dennis Lord's only problem was how to start the machine when he was sitting in one of the observation pods. Damn it; shouldn't have paid off that night-watchman until I was up in the air.

On the verge of succumbing to despair, Dennis Lord cast around. The streets that bordered the square along two of its edges were deserted. The pub on the corner was boarded up and forgotten, like so many hostelries in these days of cheap supermarket booze – Only got myself to blame, he thought bitterly. Nah, fuck it; I've made a fucking fortune from 2-for-1 deals on plonko collapso.

As luck would have it, a youth ambled into view. Bespectacled and wearing a hooded jacket – he looks like a softy trying to look hard, Dennis Lord sneered. Back in his day, he would have flushed the likes of this specky git down the bog. Once he'd relieved him of his dinner money, of course. Oh, well. He would have to do, he supposed.

"Oi, mate!" he beckoned the kid over. "Want to earn a swift tenner? Nothing pervy, mind."

The specky git, it turned out, didn't take much persuasion. It seemed he was heading directly toward the loudmouth supermarket mogul waving cash about.

Callum Phillips stood in front of Dennis Lord and made eye contact.

"Here, take it!" Lord brandished the banknote. Callum Phillips ignored the cash and continued to stare. Dennis Lord found the boy's gaze unsettling.

"I said nothing pervy," he stammered, his throat suddenly dry.

One of Callum's eyebrows raised above the frame of his glasses as he watched the Goat Man sneak up behind their next victim. The Goat Man dropped a noose, a loop of washing-line around Dennis Lord's neck and pulled it tight before Dennis Lord registered what was happening. Startled, Lord clutched at the line, his eyes already starting to bulge.

"Don't struggle," breathed a voice in his ear. "It won't strangle you if you don't struggle."

***

Logger and Dogger were knackered from lugging bin bags of horse manure around the borough and now to the town centre.

"I thought we were going to spread all this shit at CostBosters," Dogger whined.

Logger shook his head. "We tried making a mess of the supermarket, remember. Didn't work. Boss wants us to go for the main man himself."

"He called and told you that, did he?"

Logger squirmed. "Words to that effect. Any road, Bonk says he'll be in the square, playing with that fucking wheel."

155

"The Dedley Eye!" Dogger declaimed dramatically.

"Dedley fucking Eyesore, more like," said Logger. "I mean, what will you see when you get to the top? Still this fucking shithole! And then the wheel brings you down again – literally and – whatsit – figuratively, and plonks you back in the shithole. All it does is remind you you live in a shithole. Nothing but shithole as far as the eye can see."

"Coo," Dogger marvelled. "You'm a bit of a brainy git at times, ain't you, Log?"

Logger scowled and made a fist. "You tell anybody and I'll—"

"Hold up," Dogger interrupted Logger's threat. "Something's up."

They had reached the square. The wheel was uncovered and gleaming – an impressive sight, close up – if you like that kind of thing. A framework of white tubing crisscrossed against the sky.

"Is that – it is!" Dogger gasped. "It's Callum!"

"Ssh!" Logger urged. "Let's hang back and see what he's up to."

But it was too late; they had been seen. Callum extended his arm to point them out. The youths cowered, frozen in fear, as a tall figure with the head of a goat stalked toward them, silhouetted against the brightness of the wheel.

***

"Fucking hell!" Stevens stopped in his tracks. Pattimore, at his elbow, echoed his words. Before them, the Dedley Eye, fully illuminated, cast a web of shadows across the square. At the ten and two o'clock positions, two figures were tied by their arms and legs to the brackets of a couple of the observation pods. At the base, a third figure was lashed to a perpendicular strut.

"It's Dennis Lord!" said Pattimore. "I recognise him from the papers."

"And them two look like the kids from the supermarket CCTV," said Stevens. Pattimore was impressed.

"Good eye," he said.

"Dunno until I've had a ride on it," Stevens sniffed.

"Well, I'll be blown!" Harry Henry joined them. "What's this then? A rehearsal for tomorrow's unveiling?"

"I wouldn't think so," said Pattimore. "Considering how the star performer appears to be covered in horseshit."

Harry Henry took this on board. "Um, we should do something, perhaps?"

"Too bloody right!" said Stevens. He marched toward the wheel. "This is the police! Come down from there at fucking once, you fucking hooligans."

"We can't!" cried Logger. "We'm tied up."

"I want my mom," said Dogger.

Stevens turned his attention to the man at the base. "You, mate; can you get them kids down?"

Dennis Lord glowered at the idiot detective. "I'm a bit tied up myself, you fucking shithead."

"Steady!" said Stevens as he waved his i.d in Dennis Lord's face. "I didn't get this in a box of bongo puffs from your fucking shop. Now, if I push this button, the wheel'll go round and the kids'll come down, right?"

"NO!" Dennis Lord screamed. "Keep the fuck away from that button!"

Stevens's moustache curled in amusement. "Why?"

"I'm begging you!" Dennis Lord sobbed. "Look! Look at me! Don't press that button!"

Pattimore approached. "Shit. See, his legs are tied to the strut, his arms and his neck are tied to the rim of the wheel."

"And?" said Stevens, his fingertip dangerously close to the inviting red light.

"If the wheel goes around, he'll be – torn apart!" Pattimore gasped. He knocked Stevens's hand away and gave the detective inspector a shove for good measure.

"Thank you, thank you," Dennis Lord gasped in relief.

"Um, guys?" Harry Henry called for their attention. He was pointing at the roof of Dedley's art gallery and museum, a building clad in red tiles, visible through the spokes of the wheel. A pentagram had been scrawled on it by aerosol paint. "He's here! Baphomet!"

"Don't be so fucking saft," Stevens rounded on him. "There ain't no such thing."

"Um," said Harry Henry, backing away. "I think you'll find there is."

"Ben…" Pattimore tugged a tan leather sleeve.

Stevens pulled his arm free of Pattimore's clutches and was about to give the detective constable a mouthful when he saw where his colleagues were pointing.

From behind the base of the Dedley Eye, a horned figure emerged, tall and bedraggled. The boys above and Dennis Lord below all cried out in terror.

"It's him!" Dennis Lord stammered. "It's him!"

"Fuck me," said Stevens.

The horned man held his arms aloft. The detectives flinched. The horned man threw back his head and laughed.

"Welcome, new acolytes! You are just in time to bear witness to the offering I make."

"I didn't think he'd speak English," whispered Pattimore.

"They always do in the films," said Stevens. "And they'm always scared to death of Latin. Shout a bit of Latin at him; go on!"

"I don't know any," said Pattimore. "You, Harry?"

Harry Henry shrugged. "Quattro staggione?"

"That's a pizza, you prat," said Stevens. "Hoi, you horny goat bastard. Get them kids down off of that wheel."

The horny goat bastard paid Stevens no heed. He turned slowly and gestured to his disciple, a young man in a hoodie and spectacles. Hands together, Callum bowed and stepped toward the red button.

"NO!" cried Pattimore. "Don't do it! Step away from the button!"

Callum hesitated.

"Continue, my boy," said the Goat Man in even tones. "All shall be well."

"This is the police!" shouted Pattimore. "Move away from the button."

"Help me!" cried Dennis Lord, his eyes wide and fixed on the hooded boy.

There was a roll of thunder. Everyone looked at the sky, which was clear. Another roll.

"Fucking hell!" cried Logger, trying to point over their heads. "What the FUCK is that?"

Behind the detectives, on the top of the wall that bordered the other two sides of the square, another hooded figure had appeared. A monk in long habit, his face hidden in the cowl, gestured to the Goat Man.

"Brother," said the monk in sonorous tones, "you have done well."

The Goat Man brimmed with pride and bowed his head in deference.

"But you must let these people go. Release them at once!"

"Never!" the Goat Man bleated. "The offering must be made."

"And so mote it be," said the mysterious monk. "Release these people and accept me in their place."

The Goat Man thought about it and seemed to come around to the idea. The sacrifice of a holy man would rack him up more brownie points with the Dark Master.

"So mote it be!" he cried. He nodded to Callum who, with the assistance of Stevens and Pattimore untied Dennis Lord. Pattimore pressed the button and the great wheel began to turn. When each boy was within reach, he stopped it again, so Dogger, and then Logger, could be set free.

"That was well cool," Dogger enthused. "Apart from the being in danger of our lives and all the rest of it."

"Prick," grumbled Logger.

"Don't go anywhere, lads," Pattimore advised them. "We're going to need to talk to you. Harry, keep an eye on this pair."

"Pleasure," said Harry Henry. He pushed his glasses up the bridge of his nose.

Logger and Dogger slunk over, having the good sense to look downcast.

"Now," the Goat Man appealed to the monk who, in the interim, had come down from the roof and joined the others in the square. "Take your place."

Pattimore, rumbling what was going on, caught the monk by the cuff. "No, Davey; don't do it."

Brough didn't reply. He pulled himself away and stepped toward the wheel.

"Fucking hell, Jason," said Miller, surprising him with her sudden appearance. "You'm not going to let him do it, am you?"

She shoved a sheet of metal at him; he recognised it as something used to create the effect of thunder in stage plays. Miller drew a gun and levelled it at the bloke with the horns.

"Don't you move a fucking muscle!" she insisted.

The bloke with the horns laughed derisively.

"I'm warning you," Miller shouted, her voice more than a little shrill.

"It's all right, Mel," the monk turned to look at her. "Where the fuck did you get the gun?"

Miller rolled her eyes. "Where the fuck did you get the fancy dress?" she snapped. "Sir."

Brough nodded. He'd picked up the habit and the thunder sheet from the DICWADS, courtesy of their hip-hop production of *Murder in the Cathedral* and so he assumed Miller had helped herself to a prop of her own.

"But that's not even a real—" he stopped himself. Miller took another step toward the Goat Man.

"Get your hands up, mother fucker," she said. She'd seen it in a film but in her Dedley accent it lacked the appropriate menace.

All the same, the Goat Man backed away. He raised his hands again, but this time with an air of surrender.

Callum Phillips sprang forward. "The offering must be made!"

He looped the washing-line around the Goat Man's legs and lashed him to the strut only recently vacated by Dennis Lord.

"That's it, kiddo," Dennis Lord cheered him on, "See how he likes it."

"My boy!" the Goat Man stammered. "What are you doing?"

"The offering must be made," urged Callum Phillips a second time. He pressed the red button. The wheel began to turn.

"No!" everyone shouted.

The wheel turned unhindered. Accordion music played softly and a pre-recorded voice said "*Sur la gauche vous verrez la tour Eiffel*".

"Bloody cheating Frog bastards!" cried Dennis Lord. "No wonder the fucking thing was so cheap."

The Goat Man, who had ducked when the mechanism was activated, stood tall and laughed with relief.

"It is a miracle!" he exclaimed.

"No!" cried Callum. "The offering—"

He stopped. He gaped in horror as the Goat Man's horns were caught in the rim of the wheel.

"Help!" the Goat Man bleated in panic. "Help me! Someone!"

Brough rushed forward, lunging for the red button. He pressed it and pressed it several times but the wheel would not stop.

"French bastards," muttered Dennis Lord.

The Goat Man screamed but his scream was short-lived. He fell silent when his head was torn off and carried up into the air. Miller and the boys screamed too. Stevens threw up on his own loafers.

The wheel spun faster and faster, shaking on its moorings.

"David!" Miller yelled. "Get away from there!"

But Brough kept pressing the off switch, to no avail.

The struts began to strain as the wheel, now a spinning blur, picked up more and more speed. Rivets began to pop and fly across the square.

"Davey!" cried Pattimore. He launched himself at Brough, and tackled him to the ground, pinning him there while the wheel threatened to break free. The Goat Man's head was thrown clear, flying from the scene to land in someone's garden two miles away.

"WHAT THE BASTARD BLUE FUCK IS GOING ON?" boomed Chief Inspector Wheeler arriving on the scene. She was standing in a supermarket trolley that was being pushed by security guard Charlie West.

"We, um, found the killer, Chief," said Harry Henry. Wheeler glared at him.

"Someone stop that fucking thing before it gets loose and flattens the town." She glared at Dennis Lord. "This is all on your head, you fucking wanker."

Dennis Lord bristled. "You can't talk to me like that."

"Oh, no?" said Karen Wheeler. "I've got divorce papers in a drawer that tell me otherwise. Now get the fuck out of our way, you spindle-dicked spider-fucker."

The team was stunned by this revelation. It was Charlie West who took action. He sprinted to the wheel, leaping over the prostrated bodies of Pattimore and Brough and, with a flick of his wrist, skimmed his peaked hat into the heart of the machinery. The gears ground up the hat but it was enough to choke the machinery and bring the wheel to a juddering halt. Smoke coiled from its innards. Silence fell over the scene.

"Right." It was Wheeler who broke the silence with a clap of her hands. "I want this area sealed off. Get everybody down the nick. We can sort out who's done what to whom in the morning. Fuck sake! What a fucking mess!"

Pattimore climbed off Brough and helped him to his feet.

"Thanks," said Brough, taking off his hood.

"Any time," Pattimore smiled.

"Get a room," muttered Miller.

18.

Miller didn't notice at first. She dropped her bag in the hall and kicked off her shoes. She padded through to the kitchen, sloughing off her raincoat while reaching for the wine rack in one ungainly move.

She poured herself a generous glass of rioja (hanging around with Brough had improved her palate – she no longer bought bottles with nuns on the label) and headed to the bathroom to fill the tub.

You'm a silly cow, Melanie Miller, she castigated herself. In her head, her thoughts spoke in her dead mother's voice. Waving a fake gun around at a serial killer. You'm a bloody silly cow.

She put the glass on the edge of the bath and returned to the kitchen in search of scented candles. Those nice relaxing lavender ones.

It was only then she realised something had changed.

Her path from room to room was unimpeded by gym equipment or keep-fit paraphernalia. She turned around on the spot and took stock.

All of Darren Bennett's stuff was gone. Every last kneepad, shin pad and mini trampoline. Gone.

Miller was seized by panic. She yanked open the sideboard drawers. Her bankbook was still there and so was the wad of cash she kept for emergencies. She dashed to the bedroom. Her meagre collection of jewellery was still present and correct. She sank onto the bed.

So.

He hasn't robbed me. He's just left me.

The bastard. The absolute bloody bastard.

This time her thoughts spoke to her in the smug tones of Detective Inspector David bloody Brough. *I told you, Miller, I told you from the start. He's a wrong un.*

She flopped back with a melodramatic cry of anguish. *Silly cow! Bloody silly stupid fucking—*

An envelope crinkled beneath her. She fished it out. One word was scrawled on it in Darren Bennett's rather juvenile handwriting.

MEL

Oh, God. Oh, no.

Miller stared at the envelope like it was her death warrant. She didn't want to read it, didn't want to see his apologies and explanations, his clichés and platitudes.

Fuck him.

Fuck him!

FUCK HIM!

Now, where did I leave that wine?

She raised herself onto her elbows, trying to summon the will to go back to the bathroom. She heard a key turn in the front door and then the door closing—

Who the fuck—

"Mel?"

He was back! Miller's heart leapt and sank at the same time.

Before she could think to hide in the wardrobe or under the bed, Darren Bennett came into the bedroom, carrying a bottle of champagne and a couple of glasses.

"You found it then," he nodded at the envelope, beside her on the bed. He handed her a glass. She stared at it in disbelief. "You'd better hold mine and all while I pop my cork."

"Darren! What the fuck is going on? What's this? A goodbye drink and no hard feelings, old girl?"

"Well," he wiggled his eyebrows. "I was hoping for some kind of hard feeling, if you know what I mean."

"No, I don't know what you mean." Miller scrambled to her feet. She snatched up the envelope and bounced it off his impressive pectorals.

"Now, don't be silly, Mel. You have to accept it. I insist!"

"You're incredible!"

"I have my moments," he chuckled.

"If you think I'm going to take this lying down—"

"We can do it against the wall if you like. Or in the shower."

"Get away from me! Oh, I read about it all the time. People split up but they still go back to their exes for sex when they feel like it – but you haven't been gone for five fucking minutes,"

"Melanie! Calm down! What are you babbling about? We haven't split up. Not to my knowledge anyway."

Miller was confused. "But all your things—"

"I told you I was only storing them here temporarily. I've got a new lock-up."

"But the note—"

"What note?"

She picked the envelope from the floor. "This note."

"What? You haven't even opened it, have you? Go on. Look inside."

"But—"

"Go on."

Frowning, she tore the envelope open. And took out a cheque.

"This says fifteen thousand pounds," she blinked.

"Paid you back in full and some interest besides."

"But—"

"Sit down, Mel." He took her hand and sat beside her. Looking into her eyes, he explained that he had used the money she loaned him to make a series of short exercise videos which he had posted online.

"They've gone viral, Mel," he grinned.

"What? Like a disease?"

"Seven million hits. Certainly got me noticed. There's this chain of gyms and fitness clubs. They want me to be their frontman. They've already given me a huge advance. They reckon I have universal appeal. Both men and women apparently."

"You don't say..." Miller was more than a little stunned.

"But the thing is..." he pulled a face, "They're based in the States. They want me to fly out. First thing tomorrow."

The workings of Miller's mind were visible on her face. "So... you are leaving then?"

"Well, yes, but not *leaving* leaving. It'll just be a couple of months. Three, tops. And this is all happening because of you. If you hadn't lent me that money—" his face lit up with sudden inspiration. "Come with me, Mel! You must be due some time off."

"I – I don't know what to say. But it's brilliant news. For you. Really! It's wonderful,"

She hugged him and hoped it wasn't for the last time.

"You could come over in a few days or something – once you've squared it with work. It'll be fun." He hugged her again and then laughed in her ear. "It's a good job I'm made of money now."

"What? Why?"

"To pay for all the water damage."

"What water damage?"

"You left the taps running! What are you like?"

Miller smiled a bittersweet smile. "I'm a silly cow," she said.

***

Brough was about to turn the key in his front door when he sensed a presence in the hallway behind him.

Oscar!

Had he been fibbing about being unable to fly over for Brough's birthday in order to surprise him? Was he really that good an actor?

In an instant, Brough had convinced himself this was the case and he spun around only to be confronted, not by his hunk of a Hollywood boyfriend but by the wizened Tolkienesque figure of his neighbour, Mr Morgan. The sense of disappointment was almost too great for Brough to conceal.

"Letter for you," said Mr Morgan, almost exclusively through his nose. He held out an envelope covered in labels and franking marks. Brough reached for it. "Came this afternoon."

"Did you? I mean, did it?"

It was clearly from Oscar. The airline tickets he'd hinted at...

Mr Morgan lingered as though expecting a tip. Brough thanked him two or three times, eager to get indoors and open the letter in private.

"You will keep it down, won't you?" sneered the nasally neighbour.

"Yes, yes, of course. Thanks again."

"Only I can hear your headboard banging at all hours."

Brough was mortified. "I'm sorry – I'll—"

He waved the envelope in salute and said thanks yet again. He fumbled his key into the lock and pushed his way into the flat. He couldn't shut the door behind him fast enough.

In the hall, he tore open the envelope. Would there be enough time before the flight to pack a bag, have a shower?

Puzzled, he withdrew a single piece of paper the same size as the front of the envelope. It was most definitely not a plane ticket. At first, Brough couldn't focus on the lettering or make any sense of the words.

SURGERY

CLINIC

GIFT TOKEN

Brough gasped in horror as the full truth dawned on him; he dropped the voucher like a wormy apple.

Instead of a plane ticket to Los Angeles, Oscar had sent him a pass to a cosmetic surgeon in London. Brough was aghast. He kept his eye on the abhorrent thing as though it was a venomous spider that might go for him at any second.

His phone buzzed in his pocket. He let out a yelp of surprise.

This time it was Oscar; his handsome face filled the screen.

"Hey, baby!" the familiar drawl greeted him. "Figured you'd be home by now. Did you get my gift okay?"

Brough scowled. "I got something all right. Is it meant to be a joke?"

"What? No!" It was Oscar's turn to be puzzled. "It's a proper gift for my special guy. All you got to do is book yourself in, lie back and let the doctor do the rest."

"The rest? What do you mean, the rest?"

"Well, come on, baby, you got to admit you've been looking a little tired lately. A little tuck around the eyes would perk you right up."

"Oh, it would, would it?"

"And under your chin – he can tighten that jawline for you in two shakes."

"Anything else?" Brough was tapping his foot but Oscar couldn't see it.

"Sure! Anything you want. You just ask. It's all on me."

"No, Oscar, *baby*, it's all on *me* and that's the point. But go ahead, carry on. Let's hear it. What else would you like to change about me?"

"Not change, darlin', just, you know – make the most of."

"I'm waiting. My eyes, my neck… What else? Is my nose too big?"

"Your nose is perfect."

"I'm tickled to hear it."

"But… you could do with a little lipo – just a little bit – off your middle – David, I thought you'd love it. Why don't you love it?"

"Anything else? Get my flat feet sorted? My arsehole bleached?" Brough was rather loud by this point; a knock on the wall from Mr Morgan could not be far off.

"David, calm down. The doc says with every procedure he'll happily chuck in a free circumcision. It's a bargain."

"It sounds like a snip," said Brough sourly. "If you think I'm letting anyone near my cock with something sharp, you can fuck off."

"David, David! Calm the fuck down! If you think about it calmly and rationally for a minute, you—"

"No! You listen to me for a minute." Brough fought to keep his voice even. "I've just realised something. I'm happy the way I am. I turn forty tomorrow and do you know what? I'm fine with that as well. And let me tell you something else: I am in great shape for forty and if you don't like it, well…"

"Well what? It's just a little surgery, a little help."

"Well, guess what: I don't need it."

"Do it for me?" Oscar Buzz batted his eyelashes and pulled his best puppy dog face.

"Oh, stop that, you outrageous ham. Can't you accept me the way I am?"

"That's exactly it!" cried Oscar Buss. "I want to preserve you the way you are. I want to keep you like this forever."

"Oh!" said Brough. "Then I'm sorry."

"Sorry? What for?"

Although, judging by the look on his face, Oscar had a pretty good idea.

"I want someone I can grow old with," said Brough, with a sad little smile. "Goodbye, Oscar."

"Jesus fuck! David! Let's talk about this."

Brough shook his head. "No. I've had a long day and it's late. And, apparently, I need my beauty sleep."

He disconnected.

So.

That was that, he supposed. *I have just broken up with the world's most gorgeous man. Go, me.*

He took a long shower, soaking away the tensions of the day, both professional and personal. Naked in front of a steamed-up mirror, he appraised his physique from every angle. I still look great, he assured himself. As long as I keep up the exercise.

He pulled the skin of his face back with both hands. Not a bad look – if you wanted to go around like a startled doll.

He reached a box from the cabinet. He had been saving the product for his fortieth birthday. He re-read the packaging.

GREY AWAY

It was after midnight. Happy birthday to me!

He put his foot on the pedal to open the bin and dropped the box of hair dye inside.

Then he took himself to bed and tried not to make the headboard rattle too much.

19.

"Donald Phillips," said Chief Inspector Wheeler, once Brough had reminded her how to work the projector. The severed head of the pentagram killer appeared on the screen. Miller gasped. Stevens cooed. "I had people out all fucking night looking for that, but once some boffin in Ballistics had worked out the speed of the wheel and the parabola of the projectile, well, it was a piece of piss.

"The headgear consists of your basic balaclava. The horns are *papier mâché* over a wire frame – coat hangers or something very like. They still need to run tests but they reckon it's likely that the coat hangers made the horns act as antennae which, coupled with the steel plate holding his skull together, meant it was able to pick up mobile phone calls directly in his brain. Voices literally in his fucking head."

"Enough to drive anybody doolally," said Stevens.

"So," said Brough, "he picked up phone conversations and thought they were the devil speaking to him?"

"It's looking that way," Wheeler agreed. "Given that he was already deluded, it didn't take much for him to believe he had a direct line to the dark lord Bathmat himself. When actually, he was mainly picking up calls from this."

She held up an evidence bag for them all to see. In it was a mobile phone.

"Young lad handed this in. Think you know him already," she looked pointedly at Stevens and Pattimore. "Young fellow by the name of Logan Lawrence – Am I ringing any bells?"

"He never mentioned anything like this," said Pattimore weakly. Brough sent him a look of support.

"Turns out," Wheeler went on, "he was getting calls from a mysterious benefactor who employed him and his mates to fuck about, causing disruption, as we have seen in the supermarket and at the stables. They formed a gang – the Monks, for fuck's sake – complete with an initiation. Standing out on the school field looking for the ghost of the old prior that's said to walk there. It was during Callum's initiation that his grandfather first made contact. The lad completely fell for it, believing the old man to be the prior from the olden days, and he's happy to do his grandad's bidding. Meanwhile, the other three don't see a thing – they're off taking pictures of their bum holes on Callum's phone. We haven't got to the bottom of it yet but I understand part of the plan was to upload pictures of their arses to Paul Barker's laptop. For blackmail purposes."

"But, why?" said Miller.

"Why what? Why cause all this disruption?" Wheeler searched her team's faces for signs of life.

"Um," said Harry Henry. "They – the victims – were all involved in this academy business, weren't they?"

"That's right. Go on."

"So, somebody pays kids from the school to cause trouble around the town, in their uniforms, to prevent the academisation of Priory High."

"Exactly," Wheeler beamed. "Now, the GCSE-winning question is, who would do this? Who would pay the boys? And I'll give you a clue: it wasn't that fusty old fuddy-duddy of a deputy head..." She waited. "No?"

The Serious team was deep in thought.

Superintendent Ball came in. "Morning, chaps! Ladies! Good result last night," he grimaced when he saw what was on the screen. "Excellent teamwork. You may be interested to know the Dedley Eye is closed for good and is to be dismantled as soon as we've finished with it. Health and Safety wins again. Dennis Lord, as you can imagine, is furious."

"Hoorah!" said Wheeler. "That's one in the eye for him! The bastard."

"And," Ball continued, "I've just come from the hospital. Callum Phillips is there is a right state. A catatonic state, to be exact. It has hit him hard, the realisation of what he's been involved with. His father is with him, the poor man. He says the boy's mind is fucked – although I don't think that's the correct psychiatric terminology. Such a bright boy, by all accounts. What a waste! It's worse for the intelligent, apparently: mental illness."

Stevens looked pointedly at Brough. "You can be too clever."

"You're immune, then," quipped Pattimore.

"And," Ball seemed to remember something, "There's someone to see you. Come in, Charlie."

All heads turned to the door as Charlie West, a little sheepishly, came in. "Morning," he touched his brow in salute.

"Morning, Charlie," Wheeler grinned. "Your assistance last night was the fucking dog's bollocks. Everybody!"

She put her hands together, inciting the Serious team into applause. Charlie West turned red.

"Thanks. But it ain't done me no good. Mr Lord's only been and gone and sacked me. For breaking his bloody wheel."

"The cunt!" said Wheeler. She looked at Ball, who nodded.

"Never mind him," said Wheeler, offering Charlie a seat. "We need somebody like you to head things up at the supermarket, take charge of our operations there, keep the PCSOs on a short leash. You'll have a proper desk in a proper booth, with Wi-Fi and all the resources you need – once you've done the relevant training, of course."

"And the money's better than your previous position," added Ball. "What do you say?"

"No pressure," said Wheeler, "but if you fucking say No, I'll rip your dick off."

"In that case," Charlie grinned back, "I can only say, Fuck yeah!"

"Good man!" said Ball. He encouraged everyone to clap again.

"So, let me see if I understand this," Stevens stood up, wishing to garner some of the attention Charlie was monopolising, "Somebody made calls to some lads, to get them to cause trouble. Those calls were picked up by the pointy hat of a lunatic who took them to be orders from Satan to kill the people trying to turn a school into an academy?"

"Yes!" cried almost everyone else.

"So, who was calling them then?" Stevens pointed at the evidence bag. "Who was making the fucking calls?"

Wheeler shrugged. "Logan Lawrence claims he doesn't bloody know. Says the voice was obviously distorted. Money was left in a bin near the boy's house. They never met."

"So we don't fucking know?" said Stevens.

"No, we don't fucking know," Wheeler admitted. "Ideas?" She looked around the room. "Any fucking ideas at all?"

Outside a bird sang. In the distance, a lonely car alarm wailed.

Brough smirked. "Beatrice Mooney," he said.

"Who?" said Wheeler.

"The bucking bronco!" Stevens jeered. "What's she got to do with it? She was on the victim list."

"Think about it," Brough got to his feet and addressed the team like some kind of motivational speaker. "The mystery caller was pulling strings all along. Sending those lads hither and yon. Including the stables where their head teacher 'just happened' to be waiting for a rendezvous with a mysterious lover, who doesn't show up and about whose identity she is keeping tight-lipped."

"Huh," said Wheeler. "Keeping tight-lipped is no use to any lover, if you know what I'm saying. All right, go and talk to this fucking fronco woman and get her to prise her lips apart."

"She's still here," said Harry Henry. "Still fuming."

"Good. Go on then," she urged Brough, "But, sunshine, you use words like 'hither and yon' in my fucking presence again and I'll break your teeth."

"Understood," said Brough. "Come on, Miller."

"As for the rest of you, let's go next door. We can watch through the mirror. I know it's old school but it works and you," she stabbed a finger at D I Stevens, "Keep your gob shut and your hands where I can see them."

"Yes, boss."

The Serious team filed out to eavesdrop on the interview.

***

Beatrice Mooney's anger had subsided into a mixture of grief and injured pride. She was also deeply annoyed that she had not been allowed to go home and shower. The team behind the mirror was grateful they couldn't smell the horseshit. Brough and Miller were not so lucky.

"I can't believe I fell for his lies," Beatrice Mooney sobbed, plucking a handful of tissues from the box. "He was stringing me along all this time. He was just using me for information. That's how he found out about the academisation, all the meetings, who was there. He finagled it out of me."

"The dirty bastard!" laughed Stevens. Wheeler elbowed him just above the belt buckle.

"You know, you meet someone, you think they want you for you but it turns out they ave their own agenda."

Brough nodded sympathetically.

"Men can be bastards," Miller interjected. "Some of them."

"So," Brough clasped his hands together on the table, then decided this made him too close to Mooney's manure and sat back again, "Thank you for being so open."

"That's what *he* said," giggled Stevens. Wheeler stamped on his foot.

"But, there's one thing we must know. His name."

Beatrice Mooney sniffed. "I can think of plenty of names for him."

"His real one will do," said Miller.

Beatrice Mooney blew her nose, a forlorn foghorn keening in pain. "Morris Madeley," she said softly.

Behind the mirror the team looked at each other. The name was new to the investigation.

"And where might we find this Morris Madeley," said Brough.

Beatrice Mooney glanced at her watch. "He'll be at school," she shrugged.

"He's a kid?" gasped Miller.

"The dirty mare!" gasped Stevens. "Mare! Do you get it? Because she had a saddle on!"

He dodged Wheeler's flailing fist.

"No!" Beatrice Mooney was scandalised. "He's the head."

"Head boy?" said Miller.

"Head teacher," Beatrice Mooney clarified. "Of Hangham High."

Wheeler signalled to Stevens and Pattimore to go and pick him up.

"My pleasure!" grinned Stevens.

"That can wait until you get home," said Wheeler.

"Oh, it all makes sense now," Beatrice Mooney hung her head in sorrow. "He was always on about his school and mine. How mine was always well thought of, because of its history and standing in the town. He must have wanted to stop the investment in my school because that's what he wanted for his, admittedly, rundown building."

"So, by hiring kids from your school to cause trouble in their uniforms, the school would get a bad reputation. Investors like Dennis Lord and Paul Barker wouldn't touch it with a barge pole. And they'd invest their money in Hangham High."

Beatrice Mooney nodded. "That's what I think too, Inspector."

177

"Of course, we'll know more when we speak to him," said Brough.

"May I go home now? I must look a fright."

"Yes," said Miller. "I mean, you can go home. Can't she, sir?"

"I should think so," said Brough. "We'll be in touch."

***

"So," said Miller, handing Brough a cup of coffee; the barista had executed a perfect Q in the foam. "Somebody's big day." She pulled out a chair and joined him in the booth.

"Big day for all of us," said Brough. "The end of another case." He scowled at the coffee – Miller knew he took it black.

"You know what I mean," she said, fishing out an envelope from her pocket. "Here."

"But you've already given me a card, Miller. When you picked me up this morning, remember?"

"It's not from me."

Brough examined the handwriting. He would recognise it anywhere. It was Pattimore's.

"Oh!" he said.

"Yes," Miller agreed. "Oh!"

"Why didn't he give it to me himself? Perhaps he feels a bit awkward."

"Oh, he feels awkward all right."

"I can imagine," said Brough. "So," he put the envelope to one side. "You're off to the States."

"Yes! Isn't it exciting? It'll be nice to get away."

"Yes. And, Miller – Mel – I was wrong about Darren. Sorry about that."

Miller pulled a 'doesn't matter' face.

"Do you know," Brough went on, "I might take some time off myself." "You should."

"I will."

178

"So, doing anything special, you know, for your big day?" Miller sipped at her tea.

"Not much," said Brough. "Dinner with Mum and Dad is on offer, but I might give it a swerve."

"You should make the most of your parents while you've still got them," Miller admonished.

"All right! I don't need a third parent, Miller, for fuck's sake. I'm a grown man of forty."

Miller finished her tea and got to her feet. "Right, I'm off. Get my hair done, pack my suitcase."

"Have a great time, Mel. I mean it. I was wrong about Darren."

Miller smiled. "Thanks for that." She nodded at the envelope. "Don't go getting your hopes up, OK?"

"Yes, Mum."

"I mean it, David. Really. Don't go getting your hopes up."

She went.

Brough looked around *Queequeg's* as though someone might be watching. He picked up the envelope with Pattimore's handwriting and gently prised open the flap.

It was a card but not for the celebration of Brough's birthday.

It was an invitation. To a wedding. The wedding of Jason Pattimore to someone called Martin Davies.

Brough gaped at it. Martin Davies... Who the fuck...

Then he remembered. Jason had mentioned a Martin from his anger management classes.

They're well suited then, Brough sighed.

"To David Brough, plus one," said the invitation.

Oh, shit, thought Brough, feeling like the biggest fool in all of Dedley.

Happy birthday to me.

THE END

Also from William Stafford...

TRAPPING
FOG

WILLIAM STAFFORD

Lightning Source UK Ltd.
Milton Keynes UK
UKOW02f2036210716

278962UK00001B/9/P